Almost
There
and
Almost
Not

Almost
There
and *Almost Not*

LINDA URBAN

A Atheneum Books for Young Readers

New York   London   Toronto   Sydney   New Delhi

ATHENEUM BOOKS FOR YOUNG READERS

An imprint of Simon & Schuster Children's Publishing Division

1230 Avenue of the Americas, New York, New York 10020

Text © 2021 by Linda Urban

Jacket illustration © 2021 by Charles Santoso

Jacket design by Debra Sfetsios-Conover © 2021 by Simon & Schuster, Inc.

For information about special discounts for bulk purchases, please contact Simon & Schuster Special Sales at 1-866-506-1949 or business@simonandschuster.com.

The Simon & Schuster Speakers Bureau can bring authors to your live event. For more information or to book an event, contact the Simon & Schuster Speakers Bureau at 1-866-248-3049 or visit our website at www.simonspeakers.com.

Interior design by Irene Metaxatos

The text for this book was set in ITC Berkeley Oldstyle Std.

Manufactured in the United States of America

0221 FFG

First Edition

10 9 8 7 6 5 4 3 2 1

Library of Congress Cataloging-in-Publication Data

Names: Urban, Linda, author.

Title: Almost there and almost not / Linda Urban.

Description: First edition. | New York : Atheneum Books for Young Readers, [2021] | Audience: Ages 8–12. | Audience: Grades 4–6. | Summary: When her father goes away, eleven-year-old California "Callie" Poppy winds up with her eccentric Great-Aunt Monica and their ancestor, the once-famous etiquette expert Eleanor Fontaine, now a hypersensitive ghost.

Identifiers: LCCN 2020013315 | ISBN 9781534478800 (hardcover) | ISBN 9781534478824 (eBook)

Subjects: CYAC: Great aunts—Fiction. | Ghosts—Fiction. | Etiquette—Fiction. | Letter writing—Fiction. | Dogs—Fiction.

Classification: LCC PZ7.U637 Alm 2021 | DDC [Fic]—dc23

LC record available at https://lccn.loc.gov/2020013315

For Kate
always there

Almost
There
and
Almost
Not

Great-Great-Great-Aunt Eleanor was really named Elsie.

She won't admit it, even though she's little more than a bluster through a room, thin and gray and dusty enough to sneeze at. Eleanor, she insists. Hint of a British accent.

She was raised in Kansas.

I know about Kansas because of Dog.

Dog tells the truth. Or brings it to me, really. It's not like he can talk. Living or not, he's still a dog.

I tried to tell my not-so-great Aunt Monica about this once, and she nearly felt my forehead.

I don't mention Dog anymore.

And I call the great-great-great-aunt Eleanor. What's

the harm? Dead people deserve whatever names they want, I think, though if I had my choice, I'd rather not wait until dying to rid myself of California. People make comments about a name like California.

"What was your mother thinking?" asks Aunt Monica.

"What indeed?" asks Eleanor.

"Watch it," I warn the deader of my aunts.

Good thing about ghosts is they're so much your elders, you don't need to mind them.

That, and their swats go straight through you.

Maybe I gave the impression Aunt Monica is dead. She isn't.

Her swats would make contact for sure, even though she'd have to do it left-handed, seeing as her right arm is bent-casted from finger to shoulder and slung in place. She says she tripped on the back porch steps, but something about the way she says it makes me doubtful it's the whole story.

Still, I have to trust her. She doesn't have a dog, so there's no outside source of information.

The reason I am at Aunt Monica's is because my mom, who named me, is also dead. Unlike Eleanor, she never visits, though. I wish she would. I have a lot of questions for her.

And because of my dad, too, who did his best for four years but needed a pause from the single-parent raising of an eleven-year-old girl and her need for bras and similar. He decided Alaska was a good place for earning money and a bad place for a bra-needing child, and so he put me and my couple of boxes in his truck and drove me to his sister-in-law Isabelle's in Minnesota and after a couple of meals (meatloaf, warmed-up meatloaf, and meatloaf sandwiches) knew the Alaska jobs he was after would be all full up if he didn't get there quick.

He has feelings about stuff like that.

Not the same kind of feelings as there's-a-ghost-in-this-room feelings, but feelings, anyway.

His feelings weren't quite right about Aunt Isabelle, though. She was not better at "girl things" than he was, and she didn't think it a blessing to have some company, either. A week and a half after Dad left, my aunt Isabelle heard about her aunt Monica's accident and put me and my couple of boxes in her car to see if I could be a blessing to someone else.

And Aunt Monica? Well, she isn't the sort to have any feelings, as far as I can tell. But it's only been a few days. Who knows what will happen? I've asked Dog, but he isn't telling.

3

"Listen," said Aunt Isabelle. She starts a lot of her sentences like that. As if you could avoid hearing her. "Listen, I thought this would be useful to you."

She was talking to her aunt Monica and waving at me to unload the cooler we'd driven all the way from Minnesota. It was full of meatloaves—brick-size and wrapped in foil. The idea, she explained, was that every few days Aunt Monica could heat one up and be saved any trouble of cooking. Plus, making them had been good practice for her entry in the Minneapolis Meatloaf Cook-Off, which would be happening in the next month and for which she had secured an entry.

"Listen, with so much practicing and recipe experimentation ahead of me, you can see how I wouldn't have enough room. . . ." She nodded in my direction just as I was putting the last meat brick in the freezer. You're going to think I'm dumb, but I thought she was talking about the meatloaf.

Aunt Monica held up her noncasted hand, putting a pause on Aunt Isabelle's chatter. "Perhaps you could go out back and take in the garden flowers," she said to me.

Here's another thing that might make you think I'm dumb. I know now that "take in" means "go have a look," but when I stepped outside, I thought I'd find some potted plants that needed bringing into the house for the night. When I didn't find any pots on the back porch, I kept looking, stepping out to the lawn and into the enormous garden Aunt Monica has bordering it. Back when her husband was alive, he kept it neat and careful, but in the last year so many weeds have sprung up, she says, it's impossible to tell the uninvited from the invited.

Finally, in the farthest part of the yard, near the stone angel birdbath, I found a couple of holes in the garden dirt. There were some flowers tipped over next to them, roots exposed. I'm no gardener, but even I know tearing roots up like that can kill a growing thing, so I figured these must be the flowers Aunt Monica wanted taken in.

I headed for the garage, thinking I'd find a pot to put them in, when I heard a small, strange sound behind me—sort of a gasp and sort of a bark. I turned around and—*zip!*—just like that, this little streak of white bolted out of nowhere. It tore round and round the yard, half gasping, half barking, all motion.

It was a dog.

The fluffy, mischievous kind like Dorothy Gale had in the Oz movie, but entirely white, tip to tail. When he finally slowed, I could make out a pair of black-coffee eyes under all that floppy fur, and front paws dark with mud. He was doing a strange thing with his tongue, pushing and pushing at the roof of his mouth like he'd gotten into a peanut butter jar.

"Need some help, dog?" I asked.

The dog cocked his head like I'd surprised him. Like an eleven-year-old girl actually speaking to him was the last thing in the world he'd expected. He spun around a few times, wagged his stump tail, and spit out the thing that had been bothering him.

It was a scrap of paper, rough and torn-edged. In between the soil and the slobber on it I could see writing.

"Have you been in somebody's trash?" I asked. The dog didn't answer, of course, just sat there looking pleased with himself. "People get rid of things for a reason," I told him.

The dog had a shimmery quality that I now understand is part of being from the passed-on world, but
right then I thought it was a trick of the light, the sun
going down the way it was. I held out my hand to let the
dog sniff it, which he did, and to offer an ear scratch,
which he dodged.

"I'm not going to hurt you," I told him, but the dog
was not convinced. He barked a few times more and
then, tail still wagging, darted away fast as he had come.

I had forgotten all about the flowers by then and
bent down to pick up the trash the dog had left. The
writing on it was cramped and uneven, like a little kid's,
but there was something old-fashioned about it, too. I
studied the page, giving it so much undivided attention my fifth-grade teacher, Miss Tenzing, would have
beamed proud.

Which is probably why I didn't hear Aunt Monica's
front door open or close. Or the trunk of Aunt Isabelle's
car creak open, or any boxes get carried inside the
house. If there was an argument between my aunt and
hers, I didn't hear that, either.

I didn't hear anything until Aunt Isabelle's car engine
rumbled on and her favorite singer, Glen Campbell,
started crooning out the speakers, promising that the
Wichita lineman was still on the line.

I listened then.

Heard the windup sound of a car in reverse.

The shifted pitch of that same car driving away.

Glen Campbell's promises getting fainter and fainter.

I listened and listened and listened, long past there being anything to listen to.

Aunt Monica called me inside after that. Had me stand up straight in front of her and turn around a couple of times, like she had to see the whole of me to understand what had just happened to her.

"Can you drive a stick shift?" she asked.

"I'm eleven," I told her. When you are tall and need a bra that is not just for training, a lot of people expect you to do stuff you can't. Like in fifth grade Miss Tenzing expected me to be a Class Leader and not do all the stupid stuff that other kids do.

I do a lot of stupid stuff.

I feel like I should warn you about that.

Miss Tenzing got impatient with me at first about the stupid stuff, like falling asleep in Language Arts and swiping the good parts out of other people's lunches, and also about my printing, which she said looked like someone had broken all my hand bones and replaced them with chicken feet.

To be fair, she only said the chicken feet thing once, and that was before the Official Meeting. At the Official Meeting her face turned kind of pale and sorry. And after that she had me eat lunch with her sometimes and showed me this special pen she had with a slanty silver tip and how you could dip that slanty silver tip into a bottle of rich blue ink and make the prettiest letters just by learning a few different kinds of lines and taking your time on it.

Mostly, I'm not so great at taking my time on stuff, but this was different. I learned about making slow downstrokes and slow upstrokes and curves and swirls that look like speed itself, but they take time too. You ever see a picture of the Declaration of Independence and the fancy writing on that? I don't write as fine as any Founding Father, but by the end of the school year I wasn't making chicken foot writing anymore. And Miss Tenzing had me address all the envelopes for all the parents for the graduation talent show, and at the show she made an announcement about how I was the one who'd done that and calligraphy was my talent. I would have liked to have heard her say it, but Dad had some friends over for beers after work, and people told me about what Miss Tenzing said the next day, which was pretty much the same.

Anyway, I told Aunt Monica how I couldn't drive. And then I had to answer how I couldn't cook and wasn't too good at cleaning, either, and then, for the first time, Eleanor dusted into the room.

"Pray tell, what are your talents?" she said.

Now, I can't really tell you why, when Eleanor showed up, I didn't run or jump or scream or say something to Aunt Monica. It's not like I'd had prior ghost experience.

It's just that, maybe, living with my dad for so long, I've gotten used to strangers popping up out of no place. A lady friend or a guy from work who'd had too many and needed a couch to sleep on. Sometimes my dad introduces me and sometimes he just says "Don't mind him." Either way, I understand these people won't be around long, and once they're gone, we won't mention them again. They didn't even come up during the Official Meeting. We just talked about me cracking against the kitchen counter like the force behind that was my own.

Or maybe Eleanor's accent was so intimidating I barely noticed her being transparent. Anyway, she showed up and asked what my talents were, and all I could do was answer.

"I can do calligraphy," I told them both.

Aunt Monica looked doubtful, but my boxes were

right there in the kitchen, so I fetched out the pen that Miss Tenzing gave me on the last day of school and the blue bottle ink and the pad of paper with the pale gray lines, and I wrote out the first thing that came to me, which was a few of the words on that scrap of paper the little white dog had dropped at my feet. I wrote them slow and careful and beautiful as a talent show envelope.

Elsie Cooper has nits.

5

People respond to talent in unpredictable ways.

Eleanor saw my writing and lost her composure.

Those were the words she used later. "Forgive me, I lost my composure."

Which turns out to be another way of saying "dissolved into a pile of dust."

There's a lot of things that can make a dead old lady lose her composure. Like if you accidentally forget the word "composure" and say instead that you're sorry you made her decompose.

Pffffttt! To dust you shall return.

That's the Bible, if you don't recognize it. Mostly, I don't recognize Bible stuff, but that one I know, along with "Do Unto Others" and "Suffer the Little Children" and "Jesus Wept." I wrote them all out in calligraphy one time on a scroll and gave them to my dad to hang on his bedroom wall. Not sure where that scroll is now.

Aunt Monica, though, she had a whole different response. She didn't smile or anything, but when I asked if my calligraphy talent might be useful, she ducked her head into something like a nod.

"More useful than meatloaf," she said. She pushed herself out of her kitchen chair then and made for the room I now know is the study. I followed, not knowing what else to do.

The study is a dark, brown room with a brown leather sofa and brown leather cushions on the chairs and floor-to-ceiling bookshelves. There was a white cardboard box on the floor under the desk, about the same size as the one I packed my clothes in, except hers had IMPORTANT—FAMILY written on it, and one of the corners was crunched up like it had been dropped from a fair height.

She pointed to a row of books on a high shelf and asked me to take one down, being careful not to disturb anything else. She had particular concerns about me disturbing a gray shoe box, and she held her good hand to it, just in case.

She needn't have worried. I've been getting things off

high shelves ever since I sprouted up a year and a half ago. If Eleanor had been there, I might have told her it was another of my talents, but she was still a dust pile on the kitchen floor, so I stayed quiet.

Aunt Monica did another of her half nods toward the book in my hands. "You may consider that copy yours," she said, "while you are here."

The book was called *Proper Letters for Proper Ladies*. It was old, with a pale blue cover and silver title writing, the *P*s and *L*s of which were so swirly and fine a Founding Father could have written them. Didn't, though. The inside page says it was first published in 1922, which is a good deal later than the Declaration days. Also, on the inside page it says the author's name, Eleanor Fontaine, which if you're smarter than me, you already figured is the name of the ghost lady I've been telling you about.

Turns out that Eleanor Fontaine was Aunt Monica's great-aunt by marriage, and at one time she had been famous for knowing all about letter writing and party throwing and having proper manners, which seems like kind of a strange thing to be famous for, if you ask me. Anyway, Aunt Monica was working on a biography about her. Or was going to, just as soon as she got her cast off. Meanwhile, she supposed, I could help her contact a few libraries to see what materials they might have about Eleanor and her past.

"If you're going to be of any use to this project, you should be familiar with at least one of the Fontaine texts," Aunt Monica said.

I guess I had one of my more stupid looks on my face, because Aunt Monica cocked her head at me, like that little Toto dog had. "You can read, can't you?" she asked.

I can read. I might not be the fastest reader ever, but I can read. "I'm eleven," I reminded her.

"Yes," she said. And then she said how it was late and she was tired and could I carry my own boxes down to the guest room and good night.

For a tired lady she was out of that room fast.

"Good night," I called after her.

When I got my boxes from the kitchen, I also said good night to the dust pile.

I might not be famous for it, but I have manners too. When I need them.

I tried reading that book. I did.

I took it to Aunt Monica's guest room—which, I have to tell you, is sort of no-colored and blank-looking and more like a place you'd have an Official Meeting than someplace you'd want guests settling in. There aren't any pictures on the walls, or on the bedside table, either, and the bed pillows are angled sharp on each other like a store display.

There's a little no-color desk in the guest room too, and it seemed like sitting at that would make less of a disturbance than messing with the pillow arrangement, so I sat down there and opened *Proper Letters for*

Proper Ladies to the Foreword page, and I tried reading that book.

> Blah, blah, blah, blah insults or betrays the
> blah, blah, blah, blah, blah Fontaine.

That's the first sentence.
Okay. Not exactly.
Here's the real first sentence:

> Contemporary correspondence need not
> spark dread nor send the inexperienced
> into tizzies, fearing a gaffe in style or
> custom which insults the receiver or betrays
> the writer as a rube, since charming, artless,
> effective letter writing is within reach for
> all who consult this most recent of Mrs.
> Fontaine's guides to poise and propriety.

I had to read that sentence four times before it made any sense at all. Just in case you don't have patience for four-time reading, it mostly says, "Don't worry if you don't know how to write letters, this book will teach you."

Even if a person does have patience, they should not have to read a sentence four times.

A sentence should be written so a person can understand it right off. Maybe a second read if you get distracted by a television or some talking, or if you can't help thinking how you're in a strange room in a strange house and wondering how far away Alaska is.

But not four times.

A four-times sentence like that will set a person to detonate.

That's what Miss Tenzing used to call that feeling you get where you have to move or shout or throw something. After the Official Meeting we made a whole secret hand signal about that feeling, and if I made the signal, she would send me on an errand to the school office or the library so I could walk it out a little.

There wasn't anybody to give that signal to in Aunt Monica's guest room, so I had to give myself an errand of going back outside to the garden, where, if I did shout, probably I wouldn't scare Aunt Monica so much.

The yard was dark, but enough neighbors had porch lights on for me to see my way down the back steps and out to the cool grass. I wondered if it was dark in Alaska, too. And if the grass there was cool, or if there'd be snow on the ground even though it was June. I was standing there, wondering that, when that dog showed up again— this time so quiet I didn't even notice until he was already lying at my feet, his little gaspy dog breath shuddering on my toes.

"Well, hey, Dog," I said. I said it quiet so I wouldn't spook him.

Dog wagged his tail and looked up at me like I was the best person he'd seen in forever. It's a nice thing being looked at like that. Could even make you cry if you were that kind of person.

Mostly, though, it made me want to pet him.

I wanted to scoop him up and hold him tight and pet him like Dorothy Gale does her Toto when she finds him after her house crash. But instead, real slow, I put my hand out for sniffing again and made myself as small as I could.

He sniffed.

"Good dog," I said, real soft. "Good dog. It's good to see you again."

Saying stuff like that is how you make somebody feel welcome.

Dog did feel welcome. I could tell. His tail wagged and he crawled himself closer. I put my other hand out for sniffing too, and Dog kept on wagging.

"Could I pet you, Dog?" I asked. "Would that be okay? Would it be okay if I pet you?"

Like I said already, he can't talk and I didn't expect him to, but when he scooted even closer, I felt like he was saying, *Sure. We could try that. Why not?*

I kept my left hand in sniffing range and slowly moved my right up over his pointy white ears. His eyes tracked me, but he didn't flinch. "I'm not gonna hurt you," I said, and he knew I was telling the truth.

Slow and careful, I lowered my hand down gentle to ear level—but I didn't feel any ears. Or fur. Or any doglike sensations.

What I felt was something I'm still trying to find words for.

Have you ever been in a car with the window rolled down and you stick out your hand and you can feel the air rushing past and you push just a little against it and it feels almost solid and almost not?

It felt like that.

And you know how it is when the car stops and that feeling disappears on you?

I mean, I couldn't help but be startled by an almost-there dog, and I must have gasped or shouted or done something that scared him, because he bolted. Which is how I knew he was smart, that dog. Stepping away when somebody touches you wrong? That's smart, and I didn't blame him for it, even though I wished he'd stayed.

I called for him a couple of times just in case he was still in hearing range, but he didn't come.

I stood quiet, but he didn't come then, either.

Eventually the cool of the grass got cold and I turned around to head inside, and something crunched under my bare foot. It was another paper scrap, which it seemed like Dog must have brought special for me.

"Thank you, Dog," I said. Told you I have manners.

Back in Aunt Monica's no-color guest room, I unfolded that scrap and found the sentences on it. Understood them on the first read, too.

> Dear Pa,
>
> I'm leaving this letter with Mr. Van Hoeven, who won't be happy to see you. Believe him when he says he doesn't owe you any of my wages. I only took what I earned and I'm not sorry about it. I am sorry that I can't see Mama one last time, but if I've learned anything from you, it's to take advantage of opportunities when they come, and now is the opportunity for me to do better for myself. Maybe you could take this opportunity to do better too.
>
> Tell Mama not to worry. The other thing I've learned thanks to you is that I can take care of myself.
>
> Elsie

7

You know what's even more distracting than wondering about Alaska? Having a ghost lady reading over your shoulder.

Aunt Monica had found a bag of freezer bagels tucked behind the meatloaf wall, and I toasted some up for our breakfast, which we ate on paper towels so there wouldn't be dishes to wash. Aunt Monica doesn't say much at breakfast, but I don't mind. I'm used to quiet mornings. Noises always felt louder to my dad in the mornings.

I had that copy of *Proper Letters for Proper Ladies* with me, and I was trying to make my way through the first sentence again when I got that feeling you get when someone's standing too close behind you.

"Preposterous." (If you want to imagine hearing it like I did, say it British, so there's three syllables instead of four: "Pre-POS-struss.")

It was Eleanor, back from the dust. Aunt Monica either didn't see her or was pretending not to, but I couldn't help it. Eleanor had on a long strand of pearls, and as she bent to get a closer look at *Proper Letters*, they swung right through my shoulder, which seems like kind of a rude invasion of my personal space, now that I think about it.

Anyway, Eleanor looked different that morning than she had the night before. Before, she'd been wearing a pale purple dress, but this time she was in something dark, which made her transparency a lot more noticeable. I could see the cupboards behind her better than I could the details of her face or hands.

"You must understand. I did not write that ridiculous foreword. That is the work of my peacock of an editor. I can only imagine how many readers he will frighten away with his pomposity."

I looked up "pomposity" later. It means something like "show-off" and something like "acting super important." Sort of like using a British accent when you don't come by it naturally.

"But allowing him his say was the only way to assure publication. I haven't seen a final copy yet. Where did you get this?"

"From the bookshelf in the study," I said, which made Aunt Monica jump.

"What?" she asked, reaching to pick her bagel up off the floor. "Were you talking to me?"

I'm getting better about answering questions right, and it was coming clear to me that Aunt Monica didn't know she had a ghost lady in her house, so I just said, "Who else could I be talking to?"

Aunt Monica said she was sorry and that she'd been living on her own for almost a year and wasn't used to people being around. "I guess I was off in my own world," she continued. "What did you say?"

"You have a lot of books in your study," I said. It wasn't exactly the truth, but it was next door to it. "I was wondering if they were all by this same lady, Eleanor Fontaine?"

Eleanor stood up straight when I said her name, like she was interested in the answer too.

"Most of those books are biographies or history. My husband, Milton, loved history. The top shelf has the Fontaine books." Aunt Monica stood up, tossed out her floor bagel, and headed for the study. I guessed I was supposed to follow, so I did, and Eleanor ghosted right behind me.

"The first of Mrs. Fontaine's books was *Proper Parties for Proper Ladies*," Aunt Monica said. She steadied the gray shoe box with her good hand and told me to fetch a copy down for her. "It is the pink one. Top right. It was published—"

"In 1917," said Eleanor.

"In 1917," said Aunt Monica.

"I did not believe that the country would join Europe's war when I was writing it." Transparent or not, I could see Eleanor's face good enough to know it made her sad to think about. "It published two days after Congress declared war against the Germans."

"The dove-gray one"—Aunt Monica nodded for me to take down another book—"is the *Proper Manners* book. That came out in 1920."

"Written between bouts of sock knitting," Eleanor said. "So many of our boys were still overseas. We needed . . . with the influenza, too . . . we needed to hold ourselves together."

Having seen Eleanor turn to dust once before, I could see why holding together was of particular importance to her.

"And then, of course, *Proper Letters for Proper Ladies*," said Aunt Monica.

"Published in 1922," I said. I might not read fast, but I remember what I read.

"Milton was quite proud to have a published author as a relative, and it was his plan to write her biography once he retired. He hadn't started research on her yet, but he had inherited a few documents and knew a little about her life in New York society and how, once her sons moved west, she filled her time writing these books."

"Filled my time?" Eleanor straightened so much that if she'd had a live-person spine, it would have snapped. "I have plenty to fill my time. There's the Ladies Aid, and the library board, and club responsibilities, and while it is true that there is less of the party bustle with the boys away, there are still some weekends at the Ransomes', and Mrs. Everest called just yesterday and . . ."

Eleanor went on.

So did Aunt Monica.

"*Proper Letters for Proper Ladies* was Mrs. Fontaine's most popular book," my aunt said. "Unfortunately, she never saw its publication."

Eleanor stopped listing time-filling things. "Why did she say that? Ask her why she said that." She tried poking my arm but just sorta poked through it.

I don't like being poked, whether I can feel it or not—but I asked anyway. "Why didn't she get to see her book?"

Aunt Monica took her hand off the shoe box and put it to her heart. "Just as the publication was about to reach bookstores, the poor thing passed away."

Pffft, like that, Eleanor dusted. Not even a proper good-bye.

"Whoa," I said.

"It *is* sad," said Aunt Monica, returning her hand to the shoe box. "To go before you're ready. Before the people around you are ready." Aunt Monica seemed to go to that world of her own again, but she came back as quick as Eleanor had disappeared. "But we can continue the work they left behind, can't we?"

I said I guessed we could.

"That is my purpose." Aunt Monica patted the shoe box. "And, for a little while, *our* purpose, I suppose."

It sounded okay to me, having a purpose. Even felt a little good, if you want to know the truth. Good enough, I decided, that if Eleanor ever came back, I might even tell her she could be a part of our purpose too. Who knew? Maybe having a purpose would help her hold herself together for a while.

Eleanor was still a dust pile on the study floor when Aunt Monica suggested we start fulfilling our purpose by me learning about bread-and-butter letters, which, I feel like I should warn you, are not as delicious as they sound.

"I don't suppose you've read that section of *Proper Letters* yet?" asked Aunt Monica.

I told her I wasn't there quite yet, no. So Aunt Monica had me open to the bread-and-butter page, and then she read out loud from it.

Aunt Monica isn't as good at reading out loud as Miss Tenzing is. Miss Tenzing reads so you feel like the words are coming straight from your own imagining, not a smidge of space between you and the people in the book. With Aunt Monica's reading there's a whole backyard's worth of space, but I can't blame her for that entirely. Eleanor's writing is pretty old fashioned, like in the part where she says she must "acknowledge the fortitude required to show appreciation for a weekend of cold platters, tiny rooms, and little Chester's violin recital, yet proper manners nonetheless demand an expression of gratitude at least as warm as the ill-timed fish course may have been."

When she was done reading, Aunt Monica told me to sit at the brown study desk and try writing a bread-and-butter of my own.

Perhaps to Aunt Isabelle.

I guess my face didn't look so happy about that idea, but Aunt Monica handed me a pen. "Fortitude," she said.

> *Dear Aunt Isabelle,*
>
> *This is a bread-and-butter letter. Do you know about those?*
>
> *Your aunt Monica says they are simple thank-you notes. She says I have to learn how to write them if I am going to be any use to her whatsoever.*
>
> *In a bread-and-butter letter you say thank you for your hospitality even if things weren't really all that great and you would rather not have been carted all the way to a town you've*

never heard of to stay with some lady you've
never met, to help with some project you know
nothing about.

Aunt Monica says you also have to mention
one specific thing that was nice, so if the food
at the dinner table was nasty, for example, you
have to say how delicious it looked on the plate
or how lovely the napkins were. She says you
have to tell the best truth possible.

So, thank you, Aunt Isabelle, for how you turned
on the radio and stopped talking so much during
the last half hour of our drive to Aunt Monica's.
The music was good and I appreciated it.

Sincerely,

California Poppy

Dear Aunt Isabelle,

Thank you for driving me to Aunt Monica's. I
enjoyed the music you finally played in the car.

Sincerely,

California Poppy

PS—Did you know that when you write a bread-
and-butter letter, you are not supposed to say it
is a bread-and-butter letter? Because that makes

the person feel like you had to write it and not like you were really grateful? Believe me, I was really grateful when you turned on the radio.

⟡

Dear Aunt Isabelle,

Thank you for driving me all the long, long way from Minnesota to Michigan. I especially liked the part of the drive where you played the music. Aunt Monica said she was sorry you had to leave so soon. I did not think I would be sorry about that, but after two days here I almost am.

Sincerely,

California Poppy

PS—You didn't happen to see a little white dog in Aunt Monica's yard while you were here, did you?

9

Tonight we tried one of Aunt Isabelle's defrosted meat-loaves for dinner.

The best truth possible is that I have developed a new appreciation for ketchup.

Once we'd swallowed all the meatloaf we could, Aunt Monica showed me how to load her dishwasher and reminded me I had some reading to do and said she knew it was early but she hadn't slept so well the night before and would I mind if she went to her room for the evening. Would I mind being alone?

I told her I was pretty good at being alone.

Truth is, I was hoping she'd go to bed early so I could

sneak outside and see if Dog was there, which I did. It was a cool night for June, and the sky was growing dark.

"Dog?" I called. "Dog? You out there?"

"There's not been a soul out here for the last quarter hour." It was Eleanor. She was sitting on the porch swing, looking out into the weedy garden. She didn't have her pearls on anymore, and it looked like maybe she was wearing a different dress than she had been earlier in the day, but I wasn't sure. Like I said, it was getting dark.

"Come, sit. Keep an old woman company," she said.

I'd been keeping an old woman company most of the day, I wanted to tell her, but I didn't, and when she patted the spot on the swing next to her, I sat down on it. What else could I do?

"So, what brings you here?" she asked.

"Aunt Isabelle," I said. I guessed with all her dusting in and out, she'd missed a few things. "She dropped me off yesterday. I was getting in the way of her meatloaves."

Eleanor tried patting my arm. I understood she meant it to be comforting, but having an old ghost lady's hand slip through you is kind of the opposite. Seemed like it startled her, too, but she recovered okay. "It is difficult to be relocated. I try to imagine what it is like for my boys, so far away from civilization. They are in Denver, my sons. Both of them recently married. To western girls." Her face, when she said "western girls," looked a lot like Aunt Monica's face at dinner right before she remembered having ketchup available for dousing the meatloaf in.

"Not a proper letter from any of them about the matter either," Eleanor continued. "A telegram. That is how they informed their mother of the news. A telegram."

"That's bad?" I asked.

"It is impersonal. And it just is not done," she said. "They, of all people, should know that." And then she went on to say a bunch of other things they should know and that their wives, if they had any manners at all, should know too.

"They should read your books," I said.

"You know my work?" asked Eleanor. Her face seemed to get just the tiniest bit more solid for a second.

"They're all right there in the study, remember? *Proper Parties for Proper Ladies*, *Proper Manners for Proper Ladies*," I said. "*Proper Letters—*"

Eleanor interrupted, which I have to say now was pretty rude. "How do you know about *Proper Letters*? Have you been snooping? Do not lie to me. I was a . . . . I've known a lot of cleaning girls in my day. I understand the urge to spy."

Cleaning girls? "I'm eleven," I said.

"Eleven is young," she admitted. "But not unheard of." She squinted, like she was trying to see the eleven in me. Miss Tenzing said it wasn't fair, but I might have to let people do that. Might have to give them a chance to understand I'm just a kid, no matter what my outsides look like. She said the same thing about me being smart, but I'm less sure about that one. Anyway, Eleanor did see the eleven in me enough to excuse my snooping—which I feel the need to remind you, I did not even do. "Did you find my writing helpful?" she asked. "Was it useful to you?"

I told her that it had been, that Aunt Monica said I had written a passable bread-and-butter letter and we'd already put it in the mail for Aunt Isabelle.

"Eleven, and already more responsible than my sons or either of my daughters-in-law," she said. "They are the reason I have started writing the letters manuscript. No understanding of their social obligations."

You probably caught it right away, but it took me a bit to realize that Eleanor said "I have started writing," even though just a few hours ago she'd claimed she'd finished the book and was waiting for publication. Probably that's because you're smarter than me, but I'd like to think it also had something to do with how just then I heard a gaspy bark out in the garden.

Eleanor didn't hear it. Or if she did, she didn't react. I jumped straight up, though, rattling the porch swing.

"Goodness! You *are* eleven, aren't you?" said Eleanor.

"Sorry," I said. It had gotten darker, and if Dog was out there, I couldn't see him yet. "I've got to take in the garden flowers."

I tiptoed far out into the yard. "Dog?" I called, soft. "You here, Dog?"

I crouched low, just in case he was still feeling skittish about me. Somebody can be nice and gentle to you one time and mean the next, and Dog seemed like the type to know that.

Takes a while to know if you can trust somebody regular.

"It's okay," I whispered. "Good dog."

"You have a pet?" Ghosts, I am learning, don't waste time walking to places.

"Shhhh," I said. Probably wasn't proper manners, but I did. "He's not mine," I whispered.

"You've stolen a dog," said Eleanor.

"I didn't steal him. He just showed up here and let me pet him. Sorta." I didn't want to get into the whole almost-there, almost-not feeling. "He's a little shy. We have to be—" Before I said another word, there he was, barking and racing and circling round.

"Hey, Dog!" I said. "It's good to see you."

"Where?" asked Eleanor—she was still peering off into the weed-flowers. "Where is this dog?"

"Ha, ha," I said, thinking she was playing a little ghost joke on me. I put out my hand for sniffing. "Good boy," I whispered. "It's okay."

Dog's breath tickled my fingertips, and he dropped another wet and drooly paper in my hand. "More garbage, Dog? That's a bad habit, you know."

"Are you playing a trick? Pretending there's a dog?" asked Eleanor. "That is very impolite."

I studied what I could see of Eleanor's face. She didn't look like she was joking. She looked disappointed, like she'd been hoping to pet Dog too.

She really couldn't see him.

Dog couldn't see her, either, I don't think. He rolled over and back a couple of times, right through her shoes.

"I had a little pup once," said Eleanor. "As a girl. Your age, in fact. He just appeared one day, eager to play. Circumstances in my family were . . ." She paused then, searching for the best truth possible, I figured. "Not conducive to keeping a pet. But I built a little bed for him in one of the outbuildings, and for a few weeks I snuck him table scraps and played with him whenever I could. My father eventually found out and declared that I must send the pup away. I often consider that moment the end of my childhood." She said it in a super-sad way, but I'll admit my mind was on her little pup just then. I hated thinking of a scrap-fed pup chased away like that.

"Did you do it?" I asked. "Did you send him away?"

"I did not," said Eleanor. She looked a little bit insulted, really. "But it turned out not to matter, for I was sent away myself the very next day."

I must have looked surprised, because Eleanor laughed. "I was sent to Kansas City."

"To boarding school?" Miss Tenzing read our class a book with a boarding school in it, and I knew kids with smarts or talent or money sometimes got sent off to boarding school to be with other kids with smarts or talent or money.

"Of sorts," said Eleanor. "I did get an education." She'd been keeping her eyes on the garden this whole time, like Dog might be in there, but now she looked at me.

"What's that?" She was staring at the garbage paper Dog had brought. "Where did you get that? The handwriting looks . . ." Eleanor might not have been able to see Dog, but otherwise her in-the-dark vision was a whole lot better than mine. I could barely make out the shape of the paper, let alone any writing on it. She held out her hand for the letter, but when she tried taking it from me, her fingers went straight through. I pretended not to notice. Manners and all.

"You'll have to read it to me," Eleanor said.

I don't think Dog could hear her, but he must have sensed something in me, and just like that—*zip!*—he was gone.

"Please," said Eleanor.

I looked out into the dark of the garden. Didn't seem like Dog was coming back, so I guessed I might as well help Eleanor, since she was saying please. "I need some light," I told her.

I made my way back into the house. Eleanor was

already there. Accused me of dawdling, too, which isn't the most mannerly thing if you're wanting someone to do a favor for you. Anyway, I read and Eleanor nudged closer with each line. If she'd had any solidity at all, she'd have cast a shadow on the page, but as it was, the kitchen light shone through her fine enough.

> Dear Mr. Van Hoeven,
> This is my girl Elsie. You can see she is 15 and strong like I say, and good for any work your hotel gives her. What she don't know she can learn quick. Remember you are holding her wages till the end of the month when I come fetch them. Don't lend her any pocket money. She won't need it, seeing as you are giving her room and board, and like I say, we got bills.
> Sincerely,
> Arch Cooper

By the time I'd finished reading, I could tell this letter meant something to Eleanor. Something she didn't want it meaning. "Is this about you?" I asked. "Are you Elsie?" She didn't have to answer for me to know I was right.

She did try snatching the note from my hands again, but of course she couldn't. "You are a snoop, aren't you? Or a blackmailer? What do you want from me?"

"I don't want anything," I told her. "Really."

She wasn't convinced. "Why do you have this?" she asked. "What is your purpose?"

I may not always be the smartest, but I do get ideas sometimes, and Eleanor saying "purpose" gave me one. "I'm helping somebody write a biography," I said. "About you."

That quieted her. "A biography?" she said, and I swear for just a second I caught her shadow on the paper I was holding.

"You being famous for manners and parties and all of that," I said. "My aunt Monica is writing your biography."

"I am flattered. I truly am. But your aunt should talk with me directly if she is curious about my upbringing. This"—she nodded at the paper—"this is private. As long as I am alive, I would like to keep it so."

"That shouldn't be a problem," I said.

Eleanor flickered. "Pardon me?"

"I mean—I promise you, we're working on it now, me and my aunt Monica, but she understands about privacy. There's no way she'd publish it in your lifetime."

Eleanor seemed to consider this. Even paced the kitchen a little. "A biography is an important document . . . ," she said.

"Aunt Monica says it is her purpose," I told her. "And mine."

Eleanor stopped pacing. "You are too young to have a

purpose. You should have a childhood. And a real dog of your own—not an imaginary one."

"You really didn't see him, did you?" I asked. It was still a puzzle to me how that could be so. "I'd have thought for sure you could see him, both of you being not really alive and all."

"Not really *what*?" she said, but I guess she heard fine, because she started turning snowy—sort of like the television when you don't pay the cable bill. Her mouth was moving like she was saying something, but I couldn't make it out.

"You're breaking up," I told her. "I can't hear you."

I don't think she could hear me, either, but it turned out not to matter.

A second later—*pfft*.

10

Eleanor didn't show for a few days after that, and if you want to know the truth, I missed her. Having a ghost around livens up a place.

I read *Proper Letters* a lot and ate meatloaf a lot, and Aunt Monica napped a lot, saying she was still recuperating from her injury, which, far as I could tell, was already six or seven weeks ago. I checked the mailbox a lot to see if there was something from Aunt Isabelle or if maybe she gave Dad my new address. I spent a lot of time wishing I had a phone so I could call him or text him, but Dad didn't think kids had need for such things—he sure didn't when he was a boy.

I went out to the garden a lot too, to see if Dog was around. Mostly he wasn't, but twice he was, and both times he brought me a garbage paper, which I tucked away in one of the guest room desk drawers for safe-keeping.

Every once in a while Aunt Monica would check my progress in *Proper Letters*, reminding me the best way to learn a thing was to implement it, by which she meant I should sit down at the desk in the no-color room and write some more letters for practice.

> *Dear Aunt Isabelle,*
>
> *If the reason I haven't gotten your reply letter yet is that you're working real hard on figuring out what to say, you can stop worrying. Aunt Monica says people don't have to reply to a bread-and-butter letter, and if people are curious about how you are doing in a strange house with a strange broken-arm lady, they will just write to you and ask that.*
>
> *Just in case you are curious, though, I can tell you that I am still thinking that this is really not a great place for an 11-year-old girl and probably wherever my dad is in Alaska would be better. Do you have his address?*
>
> *Sincerely,*
> *California Poppy*

Dear Aunt Isabelle,

*Just because you don't have to respond to a
bread-and-butter letter does not mean you can't.
It also doesn't mean you can't respond to a letter
that explains how you don't have to respond to
a bread-and-butter letter. Just in case you were
wondering.*

Sincerely,

California Poppy

You probably think I'm dumb writing over and over to
Aunt Isabelle, and I won't argue with you about that. But
hers was the only address I had to write to, until I read the
part in *Proper Letters* about business correspondence and
how you can write to companies to say thank you or place
orders or make complaints about stuff.

Dear President of the Heinz Ketchup Company,

*I got the address for your company off the
bottle of ketchup in my aunt's refrigerator. I
am writing to thank you for your ketchup. I
never realized before this week how much I like
ketchup and how good it is for making other
things taste more like ketchup and less like
themselves. You may think this is no big deal,*

but it is. Especially when you are eleven. When you are a kid, there are a lot of things you don't get to choose, like who you live with or how tall you are or what you have to eat, so having some ketchup around is actually kind of important.

Also, I have a slogan idea for you: "When life gives you meatloaf, add ketchup." Good one, right?

Sincerely,
California Poppy

Dear President of Flender's Frozen Bagels,

The best bagels I ever had were at Great Bagel in Lexington. Have you tried them? You should. Even if your bagels aren't the best in the country, they are the best thing in my aunt Monica's freezer right now, so thank you for that.

Sincerely,
California Poppy

Dear President of the Playpax Corporation,

I got your address off the box in my aunt Monica's bathroom, and I hope it is the right one for reaching you. The box did seem pretty old.

I am writing to tell you about an idea I have for how you can make it easier for girls to get your product. You could let them sign up in school like they do for discount lunch and put money in an account like that too and give you their address, and you could just mail some to their house every month instead of having those girls have to ask their dads to go buy pads or tampons. Because some people have dads who are embarrassed about such things or don't like having to hear about their daughters growing up enough to need them. And some dads need to be reminded to buy more each month, or else you have to take the money from the emergency snack cup and walk to the Chuckles and go buy them yourself. Which is okay, except that they are more expensive at the Chuckles and that money is supposed to be for snacks if ever you come home from school and there's nothing but beer in the refrigerator.

Thank you for listening to my idea. If you want to talk some more about it, you can write back to me at this address, at least until Alaska salmon season is over.

Sincerely,

California Poppy

Dear President of the Playpax Corporation,

   This is California Poppy writing you again. I was the one with the idea about mailing your pads and tampons to girls' houses. I had one other thing I wanted to say, but I already walked that letter out to the mailbox, and besides, there's a book called Proper Letters for Proper Ladies by Eleanor Fontaine that says that writing "PS" all the time can make a person seem scatterbrained or desperate.

   This second letter is about saying thank you and also about saying I have one other idea. The thank you is because I just remembered that your company made the video that my teacher Miss Tenzing showed during puberty class, and if it wasn't for that video, I probably would have been even more scared when my period came, but because of you I knew I wasn't going to die. The idea I have is that you should make a video like that for the boys to watch too. When we watched our video, all the boys went to Mr. Hatch's room, and the video they saw was about wearing deodorant and taking showers. They should have to know about girls having periods too, because:

1. *that's biology, which is science, and*

2. *not telling is not very fair to boys, who probably would be fine if people weren't so weird about things. You might think that Mr. Hatch could just tell them about it, but I think Mr. Hatch is more like my dad and would rather talk about deodorant.*

Thank you for reading this letter. Write back if you can.

Sincerely,

California Poppy

11

Aunt Monica's fortitude for warmed-up meatloaf lasted about five days.

"Are you sure you can't drive to the grocery store?" she asked, dropping her fork to her plate.

"I'm eleven," I reminded her. But then I told her how Dad let me walk to the Chuckles anytime I needed snacks and stuff.

"By yourself?" she asked. "Wait—I know. You're eleven."

I didn't tell her how not all eleven-year-olds get to walk places by themselves, just some of us, because she was already handing me money and giving me directions and saying how after I got milk and eggs and bread, I should buy any snacks I wanted with the change.

The MiniMart by Aunt Monica's is closer than the Chuckles was to my dad's, and most of the walking is through her neighborhood, which is green and neat and has sidewalks the whole way. The road in front of Aunt Monica's MiniMart is busy, but you don't have to cross it, so it's a safer walk, too.

MiniMarts all kind of look the same inside. Aisles of snacks and refrigerators of milk and sodas and beer. Some men were talking by the coffeepots, and a girl about my age and a lady I figured for her mom were debating potato chips versus pretzels. I had already picked up the milk and the eggs and was making my way to the bread when the man at the register started hollering at me.

"Hey," he said. "Hey, you. Can't you read?"

"I can read," I was going to tell him, but he didn't leave me any space to.

"'No Unaccompanied Minors.'" He pointed at the door, where there must have been a sign hanging. "You eighteen?"

I didn't say anything. Don't know why sometimes I can't say anything when a man like that is talking to me, but I can't. Best I could do was shake my head.

"I don't need you teenagers in here stealing things," he said.

"She's not stealing things, Randy." The potato chip girl I'd noticed earlier was standing next to me now, giving this cashier man Randy the mean kind of look I wished I had. "You're not, are you?" she asked me under her breath.

"No," I said.

Randy the Cashier opened his mouth to say something else, but then the girl's mom was standing next to me too. "And she's not unaccompanied . . . ," she said, then dropped her voice quiet, "now."

"Yeah, Randy." The girl was getting riled up. "Don't talk to my friend that way."

"Salma. Your *friend*?" The mom looked both amused and a little scoldy, but the girl—Salma—turned to me.

"Quick—what's your name?"

"California," I said, quick like she asked.

"How old are you?"

"Eleven." I saw the mom find the eleven in me pretty fast. She had a kind smile, that mom, sort of like Miss Tenzing.

"What's your favorite food?" Salma asked. "Mine's these." She held up a can of those potato chips that stack snug into one another.

"Chocolate shakes," I told her.

"Now we're friends," Salma said to her mother. "Five-second rule." She turned to me. "If you can make what you said true in five seconds, it's not a lie."

The mom laughed, but not in a mean way. In a *You're ridiculous, but I love you anyway* way. In a *You're the best person I've seen in forever* way. In a chocolate-shake way. "That is not what the five-second rule means. *And it took more than five seconds.* In fact . . ." She looked at the clock on her phone. "We've got to get back to the shop."

"We're ClayCation." Salma pointed out the window to a strip of stores. Between a dry cleaner and a 25-Hour Tax office was a glass-front shop with blue bubble letters spelling CLAYCATION. "Make-your-own pottery. It's pretty cool," Salma said. "You should come over."

"I have to get back to my aunt's," I told her. "I don't want anything to spoil."

"Are you ready to check out? Do you have everything you need?" asked Salma's mom.

I'd picked up the bread, so I had all the stuff on Aunt Monica's list. Seemed like I'd have enough money for a snack, too, so I grabbed one of those cans of potato chips like Salma had. If I couldn't get my favorite food here, maybe I should try somebody else's. Turned out to be a miscalculation on my part. Tax is more in Michigan MiniMarts than it is at Chuckles, I guess.

Randy the Cashier gave me a look like he had been right about me all along. Like I planned all this just to rob him of thirty-seven cents. "I'll put the chips back," I said, but Salma's mom stopped me, handing Randy the change I owed. Stopped me from saying a proper thank-you to her too.

"It's the least I could do," she said. "For a friend of Salma's."

12

Dear Salma,

This is a thank-you note for your mom, but I
don't know her name. I don't know the address
for ClayCation, either, but Aunt Monica has
a computer, and I might ask her later if I can
use it to look up the address so I can mail this
to you. If this comes to you late, that is why.
Anyway, thank you, Salma's mom, for the 37¢
and for accompanying me in front of Randy the
Cashier. Also, thank you, Salma, for saying I
wasn't stealing and for using the five-second rule
to make it not a lie about being friends. It is nice

knowing I have a friend just a few blocks away,
even if I never see you again.
Sincerely,
California Poppy

I took my time writing "ClayCation" on the envelope, especially on the Cs, which I gave extra Declaration of Independence–style curlicues. Since my pen was inked, I wrote Aunt Isabelle, too.

Dear Aunt Isabelle,
This is a thank-you letter. A thank-you letter
is different from a bread-and-butter letter
because it is not for hospitality but for some
other kindness. Thank you for mailing the
hairbrush that I left at your house. It is not a
favorite thing of mine and Aunt Monica has
plenty of hairbrushes, but it was kind of you
to send it and I am sorry about the postage
cost. I saw the letter you sent Aunt Monica
and understand what you said about how this
is a learning experience for me about proper
packing, and how when people leave things
behind, it is very inconvenient for other people.
I won't do that again, but I want to point out
how I didn't really know I wasn't coming back
to your house, and if I had known, packing

a hairbrush better isn't the only thing I'd do different.

Did you see how I called this a thank-you letter and not a thank-you note? Proper Letters for Proper Ladies *says that a thank-you letter is not just longer than a thank-you note, but also "shows your awareness of how blessed you are." Probably, I should have written a thank-you note.*

Sincerely,
California Poppy

13

I took my Aunt Isabelle letter out front to the mailbox and was extra quiet coming back into the house. Aunt Monica was in the study couch-napping, I knew, but when I tip-toed past the study door, I was surprised to see Eleanor was in there napping too. With all the talk people do about "eternal rest," I hadn't once thought about a passed-on person needing sleep, but there Eleanor was, deep in it, slouched in the leather chair with her head tilted back, snoring loud enough to wake the dead, if any others of them had been dozing nearby.

Aunt Monica, being living, slept on.

Eleanor was in a different dress than before, I noticed.

A plainer one with a tiny sprig print and a high collar she'd unbuttoned a notch. Her sleeves were rolled up past her elbows, and her hair didn't look so piled-up neat as it usually did either. She had a look on her face like she was dreaming something worrisome.

One time in class Miss Tenzing recited a Shakespeare speech where a guy named Hamlet wondered whether dead people have dreams, and as I stood there looking down at Eleanor, I felt pretty smart knowing something William Shakespeare didn't. Then I remembered that William Shakespeare was dead too and probably'd found his own proof by now, and I went back to not being smarter than anybody.

That's when Eleanor startled awake. "Is it Fletcher?" she asked me. She looked even more worried than she had when she was dreaming. "Is the doctor still with him?"

I knew by then that Fletcher was the name of Eleanor's husband, but I had no idea about any doctor.

"He said he'd come for me once the exam was over. I fear . . ." She noticed her sleeves then, and her collar. Spent a moment setting herself to rights, straightening and buttoning and patting her hair. "You've not interrupted him, have you?" she said. She said "interrupted" in a proper British way, which made me realize she hadn't been using her accent just a moment ago.

In fact, if I hadn't just seen her dreaming, I wouldn't

have known there was any bother in her at all. But I had seen, and I knew.

She was worried about Fletcher—about him being sick and maybe even dying, by the sound of it. I wanted to tell her everything would be okay, but I hate it when people say that to me. People don't know the future.

Except, I thought right then, I did know Eleanor's future, at least a little bit. And I might be able to find out more.

I peeked to make sure Aunt Monica was still sleeping sound. "What year is it for you?" I whispered.

"What year is it for *me*? Do I seem that out of sorts as to have forgotten the year? It is 1915—for me and for everyone else," she said. "Furthermore, it is a Thursday. Woodrow Wilson is president, if you intend to test me on that as well. And he will be again if our men don't lose their heads next year and vote otherwise." She picked a thread off the chair arm, smoothed the front of her skirt.

"Where is that doctor?" she asked. "It is terribly rude to leave someone waiting like this. Insensitive to Fletcher as well. Excuse me." I watched as Eleanor smoothed her skirt one more time and disappeared. She didn't snow or dissolve into dust. Just popped away, like she had from the backyard the other night.

The year 1915 was before Eleanor had written any of the Proper Ladies books. Before her boys had married western girls—which I remembered Eleanor telling me

Fletcher hadn't been alive to see. I wondered if he was dying now. It'd be a hard thing watching someone die, I figured, though I also thought how maybe it'd be good to have some warning rather than just being told in the morning how a driver had crossed lanes and hit your mama's car on her way home from staying with friends. Maybe having some warning would let you say things you didn't get to before. Or ask questions. Or let you choose to keep the chipped-up polish on your nails instead of taking it off and losing that last proof of her hands touching yours.

If Fletcher was dying, the least I could do was let Eleanor know it.

There was a computer on the desk, and I would have looked up "Fletcher Fontaine," but the keyboard was covered in dust and hadn't been used in a while, and I was afraid if I turned the computer on, I'd wake Aunt Monica. The IMPORTANT—FAMILY box, though, was still sitting under her desk. I knew there were papers about Eleanor inside. Maybe there'd be something about Fletcher, too.

The box lid was almost as dusty as the computer keyboard. It seemed like regular household dust and not anyone in particular, but I lifted the lid off careful, just in case.

Inside IMPORTANT—FAMILY was a stack of papers, mostly newspaper clippings turned yellow and brittle edged. There was an envelope with some photographs in it too, and a bunch of fancy cards with announcements and invitations and congratulations printed on them. I took everything out of the box and spread it on the floor so I could look at it all at once.

Eleanor's husband did die in 1915, turns out. One of the smaller cards said so:

Fletcher Morgan Fontaine
December 13, 1859–July 27, 1915

There was a prayer printed on that card too, and I was studying it when I got a somebody's-staring-at-me feeling. I don't like that feeling, and even though I was sympathetic about Fletcher being so sick, I looked up ready to tell Eleanor to back off a little, except when I looked up, it wasn't Eleanor who was staring at me. It was Aunt Monica.

Her good hand was over her mouth, and her eyes looked like she had caught me in the middle of some terrible act, like threatening a baby or eating unketchuped meatloaf. "What are you doing with that?" she asked.

"You said we'd get started on our purpose after I finished *Proper Letters*." It wasn't an answer to her question, but it was a true statement.

Aunt Monica lowered her hand from her mouth to her heart.

"I'm sorry," I said. "I'll put it all back." I dropped the prayer card into the box, but Aunt Monica shook her head.

"No," she said. "It's time. I was just waiting for . . ."

I saw her eyes flit over to the gray shoe box on the bookshelf.

"Are there more papers in there?" I asked. "You want me to get that down too?"

Aunt Monica said no. Harsher than she intended to, I think, because she apologized right after. "I'm sorry," she said. "That box is Milton's."

"His papers are in there?" I asked.

"*He* is in there," she said.

"You've got his ghost in that box?" If you'd had the sort of week I'd had, you wouldn't think it was a strange question, but Aunt Monica had been having her own sort of week, so she gave me the meatloaf look again.

"His ashes," she said. "He chose to be cremated, but he left the decision about where to put his remains up to me."

"And you decided to put them in that box," I said.

"They came in that box," Aunt Monica said. "I haven't decided anything." She looked around the study. "Since Milton passed on, it has felt like getting out of bed has been the biggest decision I could handle."

"But you decided on having a purpose," I reminded her.

"I suppose. Although it feels like that decision was made for me as well."

I'll admit, this still doesn't seem right to me. I mean, the decision about *me* having a purpose had been made by

Aunt Monica, but I'm a kid. Aunt Monica is a grown-up person with nobody older or smarter telling her what to do, or dropping her off someplace she doesn't want to be. Feels like she should be able to make whatever decisions she wants to. Especially about having a purpose or not.

Aunt Monica must have seen my skepticism, because she started in explaining how she'd been driving home from the grocery and seen a man carrying some golf clubs out of the Goodwill shop, which made her think about her dead husband, Milton, and how much he'd loved to golf and how his clubs were just sitting there in the garage and never going to be used again. She said how when she got home, she must have put away the groceries without thinking about it, but next thing she knew, she was back in the garage, dragging her dead husband's golf clubs into the trunk of the car.

And then, she said, she saw his big brown coat hanging on a peg and some bags of clothes he'd never wear again and a bunch of CDs he'd never listen to again and some shoes he'd never wear, and pretty soon the trunk of her car was so full she could barely close it. And that was when she saw IMPORTANT—FAMILY.

"I had never noticed that box before," she said. "It had been buried under Milton's things."

"Did you know it was the biography stuff?" I asked.

Aunt Monica shook her head. "I wasn't even thinking about what was inside. I was stunned by his printing—the work of his hand. I felt his presence. Or some sort of presence. When I opened the box and saw all of the Fontaine papers, I felt . . ." She got that world-of-her-own look in her eyes, but she snapped back quick. "I felt *something*, felt that I had something I had to do."

"Your purpose," I said.

"Then, as I was carrying the box into the house . . ." Aunt Monica waved her hand at her arm cast like it was a game show prize. "This." She looked again at the papers I'd spread on the floor, then heaved herself off the couch. She kneeled close enough to touch me, if she'd wanted to. "You might as well bring out the rest of it," she said after a minute.

"This is everything," I told her.

That's when Eleanor popped back into the room. "The doctor has seen worse cases. Fletcher will be fine," she said. "There is nothing to worry about."

I grabbed up the IMPORTANT—FAMILY box so that Eleanor couldn't peek in and see Fletcher's prayer card. There was too something to worry about, but it didn't feel like she should find out by reading a card. Felt like the kind of thing someone should talk with her about, which I couldn't do with Aunt Monica around.

"Maybe we should just put this all away for now," I said to Aunt Monica. "It's almost suppertime anyway."

"I'm in no hurry for meatloaf," said Aunt Monica.

"Who ever is?" said Eleanor.

Aunt Monica took the box from my hands and looked inside. "I swear there were letters, too. I even read one—a piece of fan mail about one of Eleanor Fontaine's books."

"Is she referring to me?" asked Eleanor.

The 1915 Eleanor knew nothing about the books she'd write when she was older, that much I'd figured out. But I couldn't explain things to her right now. "No," I said.

"What do you mean, 'no'?" asked Aunt Monica. "I know what I saw, California."

Dang. This was getting confusing. "No," I said to Aunt Monica. "I mean, um, there were no letters when I opened the box. Just this stuff."

"And what is this *stuff*?" Eleanor got super British on "stuff," by which I knew she was making a snooty comment about my vocabulary.

"Oh dear." Aunt Monica was deflating. "When I fell, I dropped the box, and I know that some papers spilled out, but Bradley—he's the young man who lives next door, the one who heard me cry out when I fell—he said he had retrieved them all."

I know what you're thinking, and I was thinking it too. Of course I was. The papers Dog had been bringing me were the ones that had spilled out of the IMPORTANT—FAMILY box when Aunt Monica fell. It's just that I wasn't sure that now was the right time for saying, "Don't worry, there's a half-there, half-not dog in the backyard who can help." Not with Aunt Monica thinking so hard about her dead husband and Eleanor squeezing in between us to get a better look at the clippings spread out on the floor.

"'Wall Street Wonder to Marry,'" she read aloud. "'Orphan Gala Brings Out the City's Finest.'"

I wanted to stop her from reading, but what could I do?

"'Authoress Succumbs to . . .'"

Uh-oh. I scanned the papers for the clipping Eleanor was reading from.

"Is that an . . . obituary?" Eleanor asked.

I didn't have time to answer. Snow to dust pile in less than a second.

I glanced at Aunt Monica, but it was clear she'd seen none of it. I believe she felt something change, though, because she took in a deep, sad breath. And sneezed.

14

Dear Aunt Isabelle,

I know I've been writing you a lot, but I thought you might want to know that dropping me off here at Aunt Monica's to help her wasn't a completely bad idea. I've been settling in some. I even unpacked one of my boxes into a drawer, and everything fit except for my letter-writing paper and ink, which is okay because I can keep those on top of the guest room desk. They look nice there.

Anyway, today I helped Aunt Monica read through some of the newspaper stories about her great-aunt by marriage Eleanor Fontaine, who is the person who wrote the Proper Letters for Proper Ladies book that I told you about before.

We learned a lot of stuff, like how Eleanor was about twenty years younger than her husband, Fletcher, but they got married anyway, and how they had two sons who went to boarding school, and how Fletcher traveled a lot, and how a lot of the time Eleanor went to fancy parties and was treasurer of ladies' clubs and raised money for orphans, which is a nicer thing than you might think she'd do, being kind of a snooty lady, but Aunt Monica says people are complicated and do things for all kinds of reasons that we don't understand. Made me wonder if you brought me to Aunt Monica's for complicated reasons too. Did you?

Also, did my dad tell you any complicated reasons other than salmon season for going to Alaska? Because I would like to understand that. And another also, would you please send me his Alaska address if you have it, because if you do, I could write to him about the complications myself and maybe he would give me some answers, because, like Eleanor says in Proper Letters, sometimes it is easier to tell people things in writing than it is in person.

Speaking of "in person" (sort of) (that's a joke, but you wouldn't get it), there is someone here talking to me now, so I'm going to end this letter. I hope you are having better luck with your meatloaf cooking now than you did while I was there.

Sincerely,
California Poppy

15

Eleanor was back, and she looked a whole lot better than she had earlier. Less worried, for one thing, and for another, she was wearing a fancy green dress. Silk or satin or some other shiny kind of fabric you see in movies. She had her pearls on, and her hair was curled in loops like the ones Miss Tenzing had me practice with the calligraphy pen.

Looking good, turns out, isn't the same as being in a good mood. Soon as she popped into my room, Eleanor started telling me "Sit up straight" and "Get your hair out of your face" and "Your feet will widen if you keep walking around without shoes." "How," she asked, "are you ever going to attract a suitor?"

"I'm eleven," I reminded her.

"The sooner you learn proper behavior, the easier it will be for you," she said. Told me she had experience in the matter.

"That's a pretty dress," I told her. In *Proper Letters for Proper Ladies* it says how if you are at odds with someone, you might get them on your side by saying something honest but nice. I don't know if Eleanor was on my side after that, but she stopped talking about my posture and started telling me how Fletcher was away on business again and how she and her sons would be attending yet another debutante ball without him. I had to ask what a debutante ball was.

"When a young lady is ready for society—when she steps away from childhood and into the world of adults—it is proper for her parents to introduce that fact formally. In this case, via a ball," said Eleanor.

"Did you go to a ball to say you weren't a child anymore?" I asked.

Eleanor snorted, which I have to say did not seem like a proper-lady sort of response.

"I traveled in different circles at the time," said Eleanor.

"Well, there aren't many balls in my circle either," I told her, though truth is, I wasn't sure I'd ever had a circle. And right now all I had was an old aunt and two ghosts, which is more of a rectangle, if you think about it.

"Nonetheless, it is prudent to prepare for such things—to be ready for any possibility. Go on, now, sit straight. Shoulders back." She tried pulling on my shoulders and flickered a little when she couldn't catch a grip.

"I'm trying to write," I told her, but mostly I was trying to cover up my writing page so Eleanor wouldn't see what I'd said about her. Or about my dad.

"'Dear Aunt Isabelle,'" she read anyway. "Oh, not her again."

"That's private," I said. I'll admit it, Eleanor was making me mad with her snooping and telling me what to do. If Miss Tenzing had been there, I'd have used the detonation signal for sure.

"I do not know why you persist in writing to that woman," Eleanor went on. "She has not written a single word in reply. In fact, I would not be surprised to learn that she has not even read your letters."

Hadn't read my letters? Of course Aunt Isabelle'd read them. Of course she had. Who wouldn't read letters sent right to them? If anyone sent a letter to me, I'd read it a hundred times over. "What would you know about it?" I said. "You think you know everything, but you don't."

Eleanor looked at me like the Official Meeting lady had, like I was stupid and foolish and someone to feel sorry about.

"You don't," I said again. "You don't know you're going

to write books and your husband's going to die in 1915 and your boys are going to run off and marry western girls," I said. "You don't even know you're a ghost!"

Eleanor had just enough time to clutch her pearls before she dusted. *Pfff.*

You're going to think I felt sorry then, but I didn't. It was kind of an accident, and also it served her right for what she'd said. And besides, dusting didn't seem like it was all that bad for her. She'd come back this time not worrying about Fletcher dying, hadn't she? And she'd looked younger, too. I'd noticed that. She'd looked younger and maybe even a little less see-through, which had to be a good thing.

Shoot, if I could dust off every time I felt angry or sad or worried, I'd do it. Come back maybe to before my dad brought me to Aunt Isabelle's and convince him we should stay in Kentucky or that I should go with him wherever he went. Or maybe I'd dust back and back and back to before the Official Meeting, before people started sleeping on Dad's couch, before my mom crashed her car and I could tell her I was sorry me and Dad were making her crazy and we'd be quiet and she wouldn't need to go stay with a friend for a while and sort things out. I'd just sit with her at the kitchen counter, letting her paint my fingernails whatever color she liked for as long as she liked doing it.

Anyway, I didn't feel like writing anymore, so I put

my letter in the envelope I'd addressed and walked it outside to the mailbox with the others. Aunt Isabelle had to be reading my letters. I mean, I was reading all the letters Dog fetched, and they weren't even addressed to me.

Good old Dog. Soon as I thought of him, seemed he was there, gasping and barking and tearing circles of joy for seeing me in Aunt Monica's front yard. Was hard staying mad after that.

"Hey, Dog," I said. "Hello, fella." Dog spun twice and barked, which probably wasn't so easy to do, seeing as he had another paper in his mouth.

"Here, Dog," I said, holding out my hand. Dog kept spinning and barking, he was so excited. "Dog," I said. "Dog, settle down. Sit." And just like that, Dog sat.

"Well, how about that?" I said. "That's very impressive. Nice trick." I took the letter from his mouth and put it in my pocket to read later. Dog watched me the whole time, quivering like he wanted to run, but I'd said "sit," so he was sitting.

"What else can you do?" I asked him. "Can you shake?"

Dog raised a paw, and even though I couldn't really grab it, I set my hand under it, letting the almost-thereness of him tickle my palm.

"Good dog," I said. And then I tried "lie down" and "roll over" and "sit pretty," and Dog did all of it, every trick, and I couldn't help thinking how if there were any talent shows around, Dog and I would take first prize. If the judges could actually see him.

"You're a talent," I told Dog anyway, and his stub tail wagged so proud it shook the whole of him. I wanted to hug him, so he'd know I was proud too, but the best I could do was circle my arms in the air around him, which I figured wouldn't be all that satisfying, but then—*zip!*—Dog surprised me all over again, leaping up and through the circle I'd made. He landed like a feather and barked and pranced, so glad he'd finally had the chance to show me his best trick.

"Wanna do it again?" I asked. I angled my arms so the ring of them would be more straight up and down. Dog backed up a few steps. Tilted his head like he was calculating angles, and then—*zip!*—he was through and tearing around the yard and circling back for another leap. Again and again he raced and leaped, whooshing through my arms, wisping the hair right out of my eyes. He was magnificent, Dog was. Only word for it. Bright and happy and light as air. Lighter maybe.

I could have stood there all night, holding my arms out, feeling Dog rush through them, but like ghost ladies, seems passed-on dogs can get worn out too. Eventually he flopped himself onto the grass, panting. I flopped too, lying flat, looking up at the sky, just listening to Dog's *hhuh-hhuh-hhuh* breath. Feeling it tickling my arm.

"You don't care if my feet get wide, do you, Dog?"

I asked. I didn't expect an answer, but when Dog crept closer and rested his almost-there chin on my belly, I felt like I had one. We lay like that in the grass for a long while, me trying to match my breath to his so I wouldn't jostle him too much and make him run off again. After a time Dog stopped panting and started breathing regular, and then slower and deeper until he was sleeping.

You ever have a dog fall asleep on you like that? It's a good feeling. It's like somebody chose you and thinks staying there with you is the best and most important thing in the whole wide world.

Gives you a feeling that impossible things are possible.

"Dog?" I whispered. He didn't stir, which was good. "Dog, I was wondering something. I was wondering where you go when you're not here with me. Do you maybe go to some other place where other passed-on dogs are? Or people? Do you ever go where passed-on people are?" I asked. Dog was sleeping still, but he was listening. I was sure of it. "Dog," I said, "if ever you're in one of those passed-on places and you see my mom, will you tell her I said hello?"

I know what you're thinking. You're thinking even if Dog did go to someplace with passed-on people, how was he supposed to tell my mom from any other passed-on mom around? I'll admit I don't have an answer—but I don't have an answer for a lot of what's happening around me, passed-on or otherwise. I guess I just figured that if Dog had this many surprise tricks in him, maybe he had a few more. Anyway, like I said, just then, lying in the grass with a sleeping dog almost there beside me, it felt like things were possible in a way they hadn't been before.

16

Dear Aunt Isabelle,

I talked to someone about you, and she does not think you are reading my letters. She says that if you were, you would write back.

You mentioned when we were driving here that meatloaf ingredients were expensive, so I'm enclosing an extra stamp from the book Aunt Monica gave me, just in case you can't afford one.

If you are reading this, please write back. You don't have to say much. You can even write back

and tell me to stop writing you. That would be
okay. Just, please write back.
  Sincerely,
  California Poppy

Dear Aunt Isabelle,
  Maybe you need a reason to write back.
Okay. Here's a good one: The person who
told me that you are probably not reading my
letters is the ghost of Eleanor Fontaine. How
about that?
  Now are you going to write back?
  Probably not.
  Probably now you are going to call Aunt
Monica and tell her that I am a liar and difficult
and you both should ship me to Alaska, whether
it is salmon season or not.
  Sincerely,
  California

Dear Aunt Isabelle,
  Maybe you read my letter and were a little

surprised about the ghost lady, but not entirely convinced to ship me to Alaska just yet, so let me tell you something else. I've also met a ghost dog.

Now what do you think?

Sincerely,

California

Dear Aunt Isabelle,

I hope that the judges of the Minneapolis Meatloaf Cook-Off are searching for the driest, blandest, chewiest meatloaf of all time, because then you are sure to win the prize.

So there,

California

Dear Aunt Isabelle,

I give up.

California

17

"I was correct," said Eleanor.

"You were not," I said, even though she was.

"She has not written back," said Eleanor.

"She called," I lied. "You weren't here then. You were . . ." I wanted to say "dusted," but I held my tongue. "You were out," I said instead.

"But you have ceased writing to her," said Eleanor.

"Have not," I said, even though I had.

Eleanor raised an eyebrow, which had me noticing her face. She looked even younger than before, not so creased up around the eyes and mouth. Still older than Miss Tenzing, I thought, but not by much.

"It is rude to stare," said Eleanor.

"I'm not staring," I told her.

"And you could stand to smile a little more."

"You could stand to live a little more," I said.

"So I have been told," said Eleanor.

18

Dear Aunt Isabelle,

See how I made that A in "Aunt"? That is modern copperplate style. This is a C. That C is the best thing about my name. In calligraphy C is always pretty, if you take care with it.

The reason I know about modern copperplate style is because of Miss Tenzing. She was my teacher last year. She taught me calligraphy and sometimes ate lunch with me and a lot of times asked me questions about stuff, which you have to be careful about answering, even with a really nice teacher, because it was not answering *a question right that got me and Dad to have an Official Meeting in the first place, and even though everybody was all kind voices and smiles while I was in the room, when Dad came out after the private just-him-and-the-official-lady part, I could tell he didn't feel so good about whatever had happened.*

He didn't tell me about it, though. He said I might look grown up, but I wasn't, and some things are for grown-ups to decide and some things are just for parents to decide and maybe we should get milkshakes with our hamburgers that day. He let me decide what flavor, too, which was chocolate.

And how's that for a detail you'll never care about because you'll never know because I've stopped mailing these letters? I like chocolate shakes. And I do not like meatloaf.

Sincerely,
California

19

The whole time I am writing to Aunt Isabelle, I have to keep looking over my shoulder for Eleanor, who is forever popping into the guest room to remind me about manners and posture and being prepared for suitors. She stays clear of me when I'm in Aunt Monica's study, though.

You might have figured this out already, but I am just coming to understand that each time Eleanor recomposes herself, she keeps a passable memory of who I am and what's going on in my life—like she remembers about Aunt Isabelle and about my dad being gone and about barefoot being my preference to shoes—but she never does remember that Aunt Monica is planning a biography or any of the details about her own future life, even if we've talked about it together. Still, I think she remembers just enough about IMPORTANT—FAMILY in the study that it spooks her, and whenever I go in there to help Aunt Monica with her purpose, Eleanor flickers a little and then says she has a ladies' club meeting to attend or is in need of conferring with her cook.

I've been thinking that's why she wasn't around this morning, when I planned on showing Aunt Monica the letters Dog had brought. I had them tucked into a big envelope I'd found in one of the guest room drawers, and I was all ready to give them to her, but when I walked into the study, Aunt Monica was kneeling on the floor, trying to reach something under her desk, which, if you have the kind of bent-arm cast Aunt Monica does, isn't easy to do.

"Oh, California," she said. "Can you turn on the computer for me? The power strip is tucked way back. . . ."

I set the envelope on one of the sofa pillows and helped Aunt Monica get to her feet. Then I folded myself under her desk to where I could reach what she wanted me to. The computer hummed on and beeped and made a growling sound, which reminded me of how Dog never has growled at me, not even the one time I accidentally walked through him.

There is a fan inside the computer, I guess, and it

whirred on, sending dust—the regular house kind—everywhere, including up Aunt Monica's nose, making her sneeze and sneeze and sneeze all over again.

I sneezed a couple of times too, but it seemed like it was worse for Aunt Monica. "Asthma," she said. "Not too bad, but dust can get to me. I haven't kept up with the housekeeping since . . ." She started the game show wave around her cast but quit halfway for another bout of sneezing. "To the kitchen," she said, covering her nose with her good hand and leading our escape.

Aunt Monica has a phone, but using it is hard with her hand casted, especially when she's also trying to cover her sneezing, so I dialed the numbers for her.

"Magic Maids," said a lady when the call connected.

I handed the phone to Aunt Monica and stepped out into the backyard to give her some privacy, and there I found Eleanor, ready to ruin mine.

"You are outdoors, again, without shoes," she said.

"You are outdoors, again, without bones," I wanted to say, but I didn't. "I thought you had a committee meeting," I said instead.

"That was hours ago," said Eleanor, though she'd told me about it just ten minutes earlier. Time runs different for passed-on people, seems like. Sometimes when Eleanor recomposes, she's years younger than the last time I saw her, and other times only a couple of hours have passed. If there's a logic to that, I can't figure it. Right then, though, all I was figuring was how to get out of another shoe lecture before I detonated.

"I have a meeting too," I said. It was a flat-out lie, and I'd have felt bad about it, but right away I remembered the five-second rule. "Aunt Monica," I called into the house quick as I could. "We're out of eggs."

20

I had to put on shoes for the walk to the MiniMart, which made Eleanor smug, but it was worth it to get away from her fussing. While I was in my room, I grabbed my thank-you note for Salma and her mom, thinking I'd slip it under the door of ClayCation on the way.

Salma spotted me before I even reached the door. She waved one of those big overhead waves people do when they don't want you missing them, and she shouted my name so loud one of the ladies inside dropped the plate she was painting.

"Hi," Salma said, opening the door.

"Hi," I said.

"What's that?" She was looking at the envelope I was holding. With all the yelling and plate clattering, I had almost forgotten about it.

"It's a thank-you note," I said. "For you and your mom."

"Did you write the address like that? It's pretty."

It was pretty, I have to say. Not Declaration of Independence pretty, but close. "Thank you," I said. "Your shop is pretty too." ClayCation was bright and sunny with long wooden tables and all different-color chairs and shelf after shelf of pottery things people had made with their own hands. There was even a rainbow of balloons over the back counter and a big banner saying HAPPY BIRTHDAY, FATIMA.

"We do a lot of paint-your-own birthday parties," Salma explained. "They're fun, but really messy, especially if the parents don't stick around to help."

I told her I understood how that might be.

"Wanna make something?" Salma asked.

I shook my head. "I told my aunt Monica I was going to the MiniMart."

"Are you?" asked Salma.

"Yeah," I said, "right after I leave here."

"Then you didn't lie," said Salma. "Come on, we'll make something fast." She dashed over to one of the tables, and there was not much for me to do but follow. Pinch pots, she was saying, were the fastest to make but also the most boring. Next fastest was something called a coil pot. For those, you just roll little clay balls into snakes and then spool them one on top of the other.

"That's fast?" I asked.

"Super fast," Salma promised.

She grabbed a hunk of clay and showed me how to turn it into little balls and then how to roll those balls under my palm until a snake stretched long and smooth underneath.

"Voilà!" said Salma. I haven't looked that word up yet, but I'm pretty sure it's French. Funny how French doesn't sound as snooty as British. Least, not the way Salma says it.

Next, she said, we had to use toothpicks to scuff up the tops and bottoms of the snakes, because if they were too smooth and perfect, they'd just slide right off one another when we stacked them. Scuffing can be just scratchy marks like crosses or tic-tac-toes, but Salma told me the best way for scuffing was writing little words. "You can write anything you want," she said. "When you stack them, the words get hidden, so nobody else can see what's there. Most of the time I write my name," she said. "Or secrets. Or wishes."

"Secrets or wishes?" I asked.

"Like . . . 'Don't let Franklin Furwort be in my home-room next year,'" she said.

"What's wrong with Franklin Furwort?"

"He's terrible," said Salma. "He learned the Heimlich maneuver last summer, and the whole school year he kept trying to make people laugh when they were eating so they'd choke and he could save them, but he's not even the littlest bit funny, and mostly he just makes fart noises with his hands."

I shouldn't have laughed probably, but I did. Salma laughed too. "I guess he was a little funny," she said. She tapped her toothpick on the table. "But I still don't want him in my homeroom, fake farting all the time."

I understood how that might be distracting.

"I'm going to middle school in the fall," she said. "Abbot. Where are you going?"

Struck me I didn't know. "My dad's still deciding," I said. It might have been true.

"Abbot is nice," Salma said. "We went to visit on move-up day. There's a lot of kids there, though, and eighth graders are big." She looked at me then. In case you forgot, I'm big too. Especially compared with small-for-her-age Salma. "You should go there with me. It'd be nice to have a friend who could see over other people's heads."

"It'd be nice to have a friend I could fit in my back-pack," I told Salma, and even though it wasn't all that funny, if we'd been eating lunch, we might have had to Heimlich each other.

"You could wish for it," Salma said.

I thought about wishing that. I did.

Thought about wishing I was in Alaska too, or that my dad was coming back for me, or a bunch of other things. It's just that Salma was sitting right there watching, and besides, a lot of wishes don't come true, and I didn't exactly want to be reminded of that just then.

Weren't any secrets I wanted to remember either.

Eventually I just used the Declaration of Independence words Miss Tenzing had me study the handwriting of. "When in the Course of human events, it becomes necessary for one people to dissolve the political bands which have connected them"—those words.

Told you I remember what I read.

Anyway, dissolving made me think of Eleanor. Which made me think I'd spent longer at ClayCation than I had intended.

"I have to go," I told Salma.

"You haven't coiled up your pot yet," Salma said.

"That's okay," I told her. "I don't need a pot."

"You might," said Salma. "I don't always know what I need until I've got it."

I told her I saw how that might be true, but it didn't change that I'd been gone longer than I told Aunt Monica I'd be.

"I'll coil it up for you," Salma said. "And you can come back and glaze it however you want, okay? We have lots of colors. Do you like yellow?"

I told her I liked yellow okay, but really, I said, I didn't know when I'd be back.

Salma told me that was fine. Some people never come back for the stuff they make, she said. They shape them and glaze them and all that, but then they just leave them forever.

I noticed my hands then. They were gray and Eleanor-colored from the clay drying on them. "You have a place I can wash?" I asked.

Salma showed me the big sink in the back and the little brush for getting the clay out from under my fingernails, and while I was doing that, she explained to me all the steps she was going to do about the coiling and using water to smooth the insides of the pot and how the kiln was so hot it would take all the water back out and make the pot hard and maybe, if I wanted, she could make a lid for it, too, and did I have any questions?

I did. "What happens to the things people don't come back for?" I asked.

"Huh?" said Salma. "Oh, well, our policy is to get rid of things after a month, but my mom never does. She says everything a person makes has a little bit of themselves mixed into it. People get busy or things happen they can't predict, and she'd hate if somebody suddenly thought, 'Oh! That lovely bowl I made!' and came rushing back here and we'd thrown it away. My mom never wants people to think we gave up on them."

"That's nice," I told Salma. It is nice. And yet I can't help thinking about those pots just sitting there on the shelf forever and ever. I mean, which is worse, do you think? Knowing you'd been forever left behind, or hoping for just as long that someday somebody'd want you and come back to claim you?

21

Dear Aunt Isabelle,

Eleanor keeps saying "I told you so," and so even though I've been hiding these letters under the bed instead of mailing them to you, I lied to her and said that you had been reading my letters. And then she asked me to prove it and show me your reply, and I had to lie again and say that you called on Aunt Monica's telephone and talked to me one of the times that she was a dust pile.

She doesn't like thinking about herself as a dust pile. In fact, if she starts thinking too much about it, she dusts herself right into being one again.

I know because when I got home from ClayCation, she was giving me a hard time about not standing up straight and having proper comportment, which means walking smooth and quiet and pretending the whole world loves you even when they don't, and how I should smile more. And I said, "What do you know about smiling and standing up straight? You don't even have bones," which made her go a little snowy. "Most of the time," I said, "you're nothing more than a dust pile."

Pffffft. She ashed into something you could sweep up and toss away. If a broom could actually touch her. Which it can't. I tried.

But now any time she is hugging me, which is a lot, I'm just going to say, "Dust pile!"

I'll smile when I want to smile.

Sincerely,

California

22

Dear Isabelle,

I do smile. There are pictures of it. My dad
had one on his bedside table. One of me and
Mom at the lake, shivering wet, holding up
chocolate milkshakes and beaming like the sun
needed a lesson in it. (That's what Mom used to
say, anyway.)

But a lot of times I'm just thinking about
things or remembering things or going about my
regular business, and who smiles when they're
thinking about math work sheets or nail polish
or making toaster waffles?

People who tell you to smile when you're making toaster waffles, those aren't people with your best interests in mind.
Sincerely,
California

Dear Isabelle,

I just noticed that I didn't call you Aunt Isabelle, and I can't remember if this is the first time I've done that. The thing is, now that I'm hiding these letters under my bed instead of mailing them, I feel like I can write anything I want. But I also feel like somebody is listening. Somebody who isn't really my aunt Isabelle. Just AN Isabelle, someplace.

If it wasn't for Eleanor always sneaking in and looking over my shoulder, I'd call you Bella.

Maybe I'll do it anyway.

Dear Bella,

I think I told you before about Dog. I've been going out to the yard a lot recently, which means I've been seeing a lot more of him. Sometimes he has a scrap of paper for me, sometimes he doesn't. Which reminds me I have to get back into Aunt Monica's study and look for that envelope I had with all those other scraps and letters in it. I thought I put it on the sofa, but Aunt Monica still naps in there sometimes, and maybe she moved it? If Eleanor could actually pick things up, I'd think she took it.

Aunt Monica and I have been pretty busy anyway, rereading all the stuff in the IMPORTANT—FAMILY box. You wouldn't think that'd be fun, but it's sort of like a game, reading things and putting them in order. I have to be careful, though, about mixing up what I read and what I know from Eleanor telling me. Like once I slipped, and told Aunt Monica about a particular Easter party Eleanor threw in 1913, even though it wasn't mentioned in any of the books or papers we had.

"Maybe I made that up," I said. "Accidentally."

I thought Aunt Monica would be mad and

think I was lying, but she said she understood.
She said sometimes she had dreams about her
dead husband, Milton, that felt so real she woke
up expecting to see him on his side of the bed.

It would be nice to have a dream like that, I
think. Not about Milton. Just about people you
don't get to see so much in real life.

Anyway, the other thing we've been doing is
writing letters—or typing them, really. I dusted
off the computer a couple of days ago while
Aunt Monica was having breakfast, and since
then we've been spending a lot of time together
emailing libraries and archives (which are
like libraries except you can't just walk in and
check things out whenever you want to), telling
them what kind of papers we have and seeing
if they have any stuff about Eleanor in their
collections. Aunt Monica can't hold her arm
right for typing, so she's been dictating and I've
been typing, and I kind of wish I could tell Miss
Tenzing about how it's going, because in her
class I never did like group work, but working
on Aunt Monica's purpose is okay and maybe
I'm developing a talent for that, too. Helps that
Aunt Monica doesn't make fun when I mess
up spelling something. We just fix it and keep
on writing. She's actually pretty nice that way.

Showed me how to use her washing machine, too, which was good, because even though I have a lot of underwear (Dad never did want me running out even when he was having a dark week or two), I'd already worn all of them once the right way and was almost through wearing them inside out, which is something else my dad taught me. Anyway, I only had two inside-out days ahead of me, and so her timing was pretty good.

But I was telling you about Dog. So, Dog brought me another one of those paper scraps today. It had handwriting on it—the most elegant handwriting you ever saw, Bella. I'm going to try to copy it here exactly like the writer made it:

Dearest Mother,

Mrs. Weston and I are having a grand time in our travels. As you feared, there are few hotels with acceptable accommodations, but we have dined with a great many of the people Mr. Fontaine suggested, including one of the Kansas City painters he praised.

I've also met one particularly lovely girl of my own age who had hoped to come east for the season, but whose companion snuck away with a local tradesman! Can you imagine? Her manners are peculiar to the region, but still more charming than those of any of the Miss Morgans or those terrible Palmers. Her name is Eleanor Fairchild (of the Kansas City Fairchilds). Mrs. Weston and I have developed a fondness for her, and I have invited her to stay with us for her month east. We will be bringing Miss Fairchild with us whe—

24

"Where did you get this?" Eleanor snapped. "This does not belong to you."

I didn't even know Eleanor was in my room till she reached right through me for the scrap I'd been copying. I don't need to tell you that's a rude thing to do.

Turned me a little rude too.

"I thought your other name was Elsie Cooper," I snapped back. "Who's Eleanor Fairchild?"

Pffft.

Dusted.

25

And then, just like that, Eleanor composed herself, years younger and still reading over my shoulder.

"Olivia," she said.

"I'm California," I reminded her.

"I know who you are, California Poppy. What I do not know is how you came into possession of that letter. Fletcher has kept them hidden away—even from me."

"Is Olivia your friend?" I asked. Seemed better than explaining about Dog, and besides, I was curious.

For a second I thought Eleanor was going to dust again, but then she looked straight at me, sort of like she trusted me and sort of like she didn't.

"If I remember correctly, you already know I was born Elsie Cooper."

I nodded.

"And you likewise know that when I was twelve, my father lied about my age and sent me to work at a hotel in Kansas City."

I nodded again.

"Olivia was a guest at that hotel. She overheard me imitating the accent of her English governess. She might have had me fired. Instead she was amused, and she and Mrs. Weston made a game of teaching me proper manners and proper speech. When it came time for them to return home, they were so pleased with my progress they decided on another game. They would bring me with them to New York to see if they could fool all of their society friends into believing I was one of them. I would be Eleanor Fairchild—"

"Of the Kansas City Fairchilds," I said.

Eleanor nodded. "Fletcher Fontaine was the only one to discern the truth, but he said nothing until Olivia and Mrs. Weston tired of their game. They had plans to go abroad and were not keen to take me with them. Olivia turned to Fletcher for help in finding me hotel work—"

"And then you told him the truth and you both fell in love and you lived happily ever after," I said, which was funny because I had seen enough of Eleanor's life to know she hadn't always lived happily. Not even most of the time. Make-believe stories just sneak inside you when you're not looking, I guess.

"Fletcher wanted a wife. And he wants children," Eleanor said. "He proposed to Eleanor Fairchild, on the condition that Elsie Cooper disappear forever."

"He wanted you to lie," I said. It wasn't very mannerly of me, I know, but that's what I was thinking.

"Fletcher sees me for who I am, but he understands that society will not. He sent a Pinkerton detective to collect all proof of my earlier life," Eleanor went on. "Letters, employment papers, the few school records there were. My father even sold the agent a rag doll he claimed had been my dearest childhood possession."

"It wasn't?" I asked.

"I'd never seen it before in my life," Eleanor said. "My father was skilled at ruses too."

"He ever come visit you in New York? Does your mom?"

"They do not."

"Do you miss them?"

"I miss Oakley," she said, more to herself than me, "but I can only assume he has gone by now, too."

I wanted to ask about this Oakley person, but I was afraid talking might remind Eleanor to be mad at me, and just then her face looked kind of tender. Like what she was remembering was so real she was more alive in her memory than she was in the room with me.

My dad gets that way sometimes. If there aren't any people around, but he is having beers anyway, he gets that way about my mom, I think. I mean, he doesn't talk to me about it or anything. It's just that even though he's right there on the couch, you can tell he is also someplace else, some other world, like Aunt Monica used to say. Someplace I'd go with him, if he'd tell me how.

26

Dear Bella,

Today Aunt Monica and I read a review of
Eleanor's last book, published posthumously,
which means after a person dies, in case you
were wondering.

Have you ever thought about what it would
be like to be posthumous? I'd like to know more
about how it feels, but Dog can't tell me, and
asking Eleanor would just dust her again.

I do wonder what it's like when she's dust,
though. Do you think she's really there in the
dust, or does she go to some other passed-

on place? And if she does, do you think there are other passed-on people around, like her husband, Fletcher? Or my mom?

Sometimes I think maybe the passed-on world is right here with us all the time, but most of the passed-on people are better at hiding themselves than Eleanor is with me.

Maybe my mom is right here too.

Maybe she's been watching me the whole time.

I think about that a lot. Her watching me.

You'd think it would make me feel good, being watched over, but there are some things I think maybe I wouldn't want her to see.

Your friend,

Callie

PS—Would you mind if I called myself Callie, just for our letters?

27

Dear Bella,

The Magic Maids are coming tomorrow to clean and vacuum and mostly dust, which makes me double glad I didn't risk asking Eleanor about the passed-on world. You can't sweep her when she's dusted, but who knows what a vacuum might do?

Aunt Monica had me put all our papers away in the IMPORTANT—FAMILY box because, she says, you never know what people might throw away without knowing it's worth something. She says we should go next door to her neighbor

Bradley's while they're cleaning too. Says she doesn't like being in the house when there are strangers in it. Good thing she doesn't know about Eleanor.

Still, I get what she means. Sometimes at my dad's I'd wake up and find one of his lady friends in the kitchen scrambling an egg, or there'd be someone having coffee at the table, or I'd make the mistake of singing, not realizing there was a man sleeping on the couch until he told me he was there trying to keep doing so.

That was the worst, always. You could pretend people weren't there if they didn't talk to you. But then the lady friends would say how grown up I was and maybe we could go to the mall together sometime. Men said that grown-up thing too, though they were less inclined toward shopping.

One time a man said he heard my name was California and did I know what they say about California, how it is the Land of Milk and Honey? "Are you made of milk and honey?" he asked. I was trying to toast a waffle, and he said, "Maybe just honey." And he said don't be so serious and he was just fooling around and I should smile and that the boys would like me more if I smiled. Didn't I know how to smile?

*It was easy. He'd show me, he said. He put his
finger to the corner of my mouth. It was dry and
cracked, his finger. He said he'd show me.*

   *And then my dad was in the kitchen, charging
at that man and knocking him to the ground,
and I was getting knocked to the ground too,
and I didn't notice and Dad didn't notice until
the next day how my arm was bruised blue
and didn't move exactly right. And then we
went to the urgent care. And then somebody at
school asked me about it. And then there was an
Official Meeting.*

   *I think I'm going to go outside and see if Dog's
around.*

   Your friend,
   Callie

Dear Bella,

Just in case you were wondering, when we
drove off from Kentucky, I didn't know Dad
was going to leave me at Aunt Isabelle's house.
Probably I should have figured it out when he
told me to pack my things in my boxes, but
I don't have a lot of things and I don't have
a suitcase, either, and he said we were going
to meet family, and I didn't put two and two
together like I should have, I guess.

Most of the drive we just listened to his oldies
playlist, and he said how those songs weren't

oldies, they were from his high school days. And he said when he was in high school, all he wanted was to be outdoors camping and hunting and not being penned up in a school. And he said how his big dream was to go to Alaska and how he'd heard there was a lot of money to be made during salmon season and that was the kind of work men like him needed. Being outside, working with his hands, and making the kind of money that would make life easier for his family, by which, I guess, he meant me.

He talked a lot about that. About how Alaska was just you and the wilderness, and a person would know who he was out there. The closer we got to Minnesota, the more he started saying how Alaska wasn't really a girl kind of place, he didn't think. And how he wasn't really all that sure about girl things, particularly growing-girl things.

We crossed the Minnesota border, and he said how in the Official Meeting the counselor lady told him that I was going through changes and he couldn't expect me to be so easy to care for as I had been when I was little. How I was going to have some hormones now and body changes, and how situations that might have seemed no problem before could be more complicated. He paused before he said "complicated," like he was rustling around in a packing box searching for that word.

"If your mom were here, California, she'd know what to do. She'd know how to take you shopping for bras and all the other girl things," he said. He had to do some box rustling before he said "bras," too.

And then he said how his sister-in-law, Isabelle, knew all about girl things and how it would be a blessing to her to have company after so many years of living by herself.

You already know he was wrong about the company part.

I try not to think about what else he might have gotten wrong.

I hope he wasn't wrong about the salmon and the money and how working with his hands would be good for him. I hope things are good for him. Truth is, things are pretty good for me right now too, except I don't really want to go next door to a strange man's house, so I'm thinking of asking Aunt Monica if I can go to the MiniMart instead. Just for milk, though. Not for anything else.

And now I'll sign off and get this letter in an envelope and make a show of putting a stamp

on it, like I always do in case Eleanor pops
in. Don't need her starting up again about
how nobody cares enough to read my letters.
Thing is, it feels like when I'm writing to you,
somebody does.
   Even if that somebody is only me.
   Sincerely,
   Callie

29

The thing about going to the MiniMart is you have to almost walk by ClayCation to do it.

And if you walk by ClayCation, even if there are lots of little kids and parents rushing in wearing party clothes and holding presents, it's possible that you might get spotted by someone who one time called you her friend.

It didn't happen right away.

I had to stand there in the parking lot awhile, dodging cars and watching all those moms and dads dropping their kids inside ClayCation and then rushing back out to their cars to go wherever else it was they wanted to be. Salma was opening the door for all of them, and at one point I must have moved or something, because she finally saw me standing out there in the lot.

I'll admit, just then I was hoping she'd wave that overhead wave, but she ducked right back into ClayCation, door shutting behind her.

You ever get your nails polished?

Thing about it is you have to be still. She has to be still too, the person doing your nails. She has to hold your hand in hers and be real still and pay attention only to you and your fingers and your hand, and both of you have to almost breathe at the same time, that's how still you have to be if you don't want to mess things up.

And when it's all done, you have to stay there a little while longer, waiting for the pink to dry, and sometimes, if you're real still and you don't touch anything else, it can feel like you're still holding hands, even if the other person is long gone.

Milk, I reminded myself. I'd told Aunt Monica I'd buy milk.

I stood there still a second longer, and then Salma was at the ClayCation door waving that overhead wave. "California!" she called loud enough to break a room of plates. "California!"

I hurried over—her voice sounded urgent, is all. "I had to check with my mom," she said, "because of the party. But if you want to paint your pot, it's ready for you."

Salma had coiled up my Declaration of Independence

snakes into the prettiest pot you ever saw—tall as a milk-shake cup, but fatter and more solid. Made a lid for it too that fit on neat. I was a little bit afraid that my trying to paint it would mess it up, but Salma said for me not to be silly, and did I want yellow glaze?

"Does it come in pink?" I asked her.

I didn't paint my pot right off. There were too many kids around squealing and spilling things and needing help, because except for the birthday kid's mom and dad, all the other parents had left. Which you probably remember Salma saying makes for a messy afternoon.

I didn't know anything about pottery or painting, but I watched Salma and her mom, how they smiled and encouraged and helped kids figure out how many unicorns might fit on a single plate (three, if you're curious). Nobody asked me about unicorns, but one boy, who had needed two birthday party name tags to write SEBASTI and AN, did ask if I would write his name on his plate for him. After we practiced a few times on paper, though, he did it himself just fine. Didn't look like a Founding Father wrote it, but I expect it would have met with their approval.

The birthday kid, Esperanza, said I could have some cake, but I took the cake time for painting my coil pot instead. Compared to all the unicorns and fire trucks and angel scenes on the birthday plates, it might sound like painting a plain pink glaze was sort of boring, and maybe it was, but Salma said once it got kiln-fired for a second time, it would be beautiful, I just had to trust her.

Probably shouldn't take so long painting a glaze as it does painting unicorns, but I took my time anyway, holding the pot still as still, and painting slow and smooth.

Naomi—that's Salma's mom—came over to watch near the end. Told me I did fine work.

"If you were older, I'd offer you a job," she said. Felt good to hear that, I have to say, and if Naomi wasn't the kind who could see the eleven in a person, I might have lied and told her I was a teenager after all.

Even though it wasn't my job, I helped Salma clean up the paint spills and cake spills and juice box drips, and she said how if I went to Abbot Middle School with her, we could both come here after school and do our homework together and she could show me how to make more kinds of pots, and then when we were fourteen, we could both get work permits and work here together for real.

And then Salma had me carry my glazed pot to the kiln in the EMPLOYEES ONLY back room, like I already worked there and was welcome. And then she asked when my dad was going to make up his mind about where I was going to school.

"Probably when salmon season is over," I told her.

"When's that?"

I shrugged. Maybe it seemed stupid, me not knowing, but Salma didn't say so.

And then I got an idea that didn't seem stupid at all.

And I told Salma thank you and I had to go home, and not to worry, I'd be back for that coil pot, and I started for Aunt Monica's, thinking about my idea so much I almost forgot to buy the milk at the MiniMart like I'd promised, but after I got the milk, I kept thinking about that idea all the way, all the way, all the way home.

30

Dog was waiting for me when I got to Aunt Monica's, sitting behind the gate to the backyard, wagging and wiggling and barking his gaspy bark.

"Hello there, Dog," I said. You'd have thought I'd told him he won the lotto, he was so excited to hear my voice. "Back up now," I said. "Let me in." I suppose I didn't have to say that, seeing as a swinging gate would have gone right through him, but like I said, I have manners, and besides, the more I saw Dog, the more real he felt to me. Wasn't his fault he was only almost there, was it?

Dog followed me round to the back porch, barking and spinning and wanting to play, but my idea was bubbling strong and I couldn't think about much else. "I'll be back out later," I told him. "Stay, okay? I'll be back."

Dog heard that word "stay" and he sat down solid, like staying was all he had hoped to do anyway. "I'll be back," I told him again.

I opened the kitchen door and right off was hit by the scent of Christmas trees and lemons and some other kind of cleaning smell I almost recognized. There was a postcard on the kitchen table saying THE MAGIC MAIDS WERE HERE, and a small stack of mail sat underneath that, but every other surface in the kitchen was clean and shiny and clutter-free. The floors were shiny too. Even the inside of the refrigerator looked neat, though how that could be, I wasn't sure, given how there never had been much in it besides eggs and milk and ketchup.

I could hear Aunt Monica in her study, sounding busy on her phone, saying that next week would be fine, so I just waved at her as I walked by, and she wiggled her cast fingers hello at me, and I went back to my room quick as I could.

All the way home from the MiniMart I'd been thinking about my idea. About what Salma's mom had said about how she could use an employee, and how Salma had said maybe I could go to Abbot Middle School with her, and how Eleanor says in *Proper Letters for Proper Ladies* that it is advantageous to propose a plan in writing so people will know your intentions are serious and not think your excitement is simply the ramblings of a flibbertigibbet. I still don't know what a flibbertigibbet is, but I was pretty sure even then that it was something to avoid.

The guest room smelled like lemons too. I had made the bed up neat that morning, but it was made up even neater now. My boxes were stacked in the corner, and somebody had even refolded what clothes I had in the drawer.

I centered my pad of gray-lined paper on the desk and twisted the cap off the blue bottle ink. I got the slanty-tip pen from the desk drawer and dipped it in the bottle. I took a couple of deep breaths, too, like Miss Tenzing always told me to as a way of slowing down and being careful. And then I wrote, neat and straight and careful as I could.

> *Dear Dad,*
>
> *I hope that you are having a good time in Alaska. I hope that you like working outdoors and knowing who you are. I hope that salmon season is good, too.*
>
> *Did Aunt Isabelle tell you I am staying at her aunt Monica's now? At first that was hard because I missed you and Aunt Monica took a lot of naps and there was mostly meatloaf to eat, but now things are pretty good. The Magic Maids came today, for one thing, and everything*

feels fresh and lemony. And for another thing, now that Aunt Monica and I are working on her purpose, she doesn't sleep so much during the day and she seems a lot happier most of the time. And I have my own room with a big window, and West Bloomfield feels almost as much like home as any place we ever were— or it would if you were here. Which is what I'm writing you about. Also, there is a place here called ClayCation, which is where people make pottery and have birthday parties. I was there today and I got a really good idea.

I don't know when salmon season is over, but I don't think you have to stay that long anyway. I think you can come right now to West Bloomfield, Michigan. Because guess what? ClayCation needs an employee! And guess what else? Making pots and stuff means working with your hands, which is perfect! The other perfect thing is that there is a middle school here called Abbot Middle School, and Salma—that's the girl whose mom owns ClayCation—she says that other than some boy named Franklin, people there are pretty nice. And I bet we could get an apartment or something, but if there isn't enough salmon money for that, I bet Aunt Monica would let us stay in her guest room for a while, especially if you can drive a stick shift. Can you?

Please write back soon and say yes about my plan so I can tell Salma and her mom that the job is filled. And maybe so Aunt Monica could tell the school. You don't have to mention anything about the Official Meeting at my old school, but maybe you could say it would be good for my adjustment if me and Salma were in all the same classes together? I will find out Salma's last name and tell you, if that helps.

Yours truly,

California

31

I was all out of stamps by then, and I didn't have my dad's Alaska address, so I went looking for Aunt Monica to see if she had either one. She was still on her phone, talking to I don't know who about what time was best for driving to a place and where the parking lot was, but she wiggled her cast fingers at me in a *Come on in* kind of way, which I did, which is how I found Eleanor dusted into a pile at Aunt Monica's feet.

Didn't take long to figure out what had happened. That envelope I'd lost? The one with all the scraps and letters Dog had brought? It was sitting there flat on Aunt Monica's desk, contents spread out everywhere. Eleanor must have come upon it and read something decomposing, I figured, but before I could get close enough to see just what that was, Aunt Monica tapped off her phone and dropped it in her pocket.

"California!" she said, happy, like she'd spotted a friend in a crowded room. "Look!" She waved her game show hand over the scraps I'd been noticing. "Do you know where all this came from?" she asked.

I guess I wasn't supposed to answer, because just as I did, she spoke too.

"The backyard," I said, same time as she said, "Behind the sofa cushions."

And then we both said, "What?"

And then we both said, "What'd you say?"

And then we both said, "You first."

And then Aunt Monica said, "The Magic Maids found this envelope in the sofa cushions. I was on some pain medicine after my fall, and I thought perhaps when I came home from the hospital I had put these in an envelope and then fallen asleep on the sofa and forgotten them—but what did you say? Did you say this came from the *backyard*?"

I'd be lying to you now if I didn't tell you I thought about lying to her then, but I couldn't figure out a way of making that lie true in five seconds, so instead I settled on telling the best truth possible. Which was leaving out the part about Dog and just saying how sometimes when I was taking in the garden flowers, I'd find these little scraps of paper. I told her how at first I wasn't sure they were important, but then later I thought they might be, and that's when I put them in the envelope to give her, but then I lost the envelope and thought they were gone forever.

You remember how I said Miss Tenzing told me to give people time to find the smart in me? Well, this was one time I hoped a person wouldn't go looking for it.

It'd be better, I thought, if Aunt Monica believed I was a dumbbell than if she thought I'd been sneaky and keeping secrets.

But Aunt Monica didn't look at me like I was dumb.

Didn't look like she thought I was sneaky, either. Mostly, she just looked excited.

"Do you think there might be more?" she asked.

Dog hadn't brought me any scraps in a bit, but that didn't mean there weren't any more to find. "Maybe?" I said.

And just like that, Aunt Monica was rushing out to the backyard, calling for me to follow.

You're going to think I'm a terrible person, but I had forgotten all about telling Dog to wait for me. Dog hadn't forgotten, that's for sure. He was sitting there, wiggling and gasping like I'd come back from the dead, so to speak.

I hurried over to him and whispered a hello and a sorry for taking so long.

"Did you find something?" Aunt Monica called.

"Not yet," I called back. "Come on, Dog," I whispered, and—*zip!*—Dog leaped up and spun and started running circles around me as I headed for the far back of the garden. It's a good feeling having somebody circle you like that, needing so much to run but determined to keep you in sight while he does it.

If I didn't love Dog already, that would have been the envelope sealer.

And it is one more reason to want Dad to work at ClayCation and for us to stay here with Aunt Monica.

Dog will be here. Or almost here.

And he'll be mine.

"Dog," I said when we got to the stone angel birdbath. "Dog, did you find any more of those letters? Huh? You find any papers today, boy?"

Dog tilted his head at me, which I shouldn't have been surprised about. He is a dog, after all. What does he know about letters? I tried something else. "Fetch," I said. "Go on. Fetch."

Dog didn't look any more inspired, but he turned around a few times and plunged deep into a weed patch. When he didn't come out for a bit, I followed.

"Did you find something?" said Aunt Monica, coming up behind me.

"No," I said. "I'm sorry."

"Don't be sorry," said Aunt Monica. She looked around

the garden like she hadn't seen it in a very long while, which might have been true. In the whole time I'd been there, I hadn't seen her outside once, except today when she was on her way next door to be inside Bradley's house. "It's a mess, isn't it? Milton would be mortified."

I looked up "mortified" in the dictionary later and found two meanings—a modern one, which is like "ashamed or embarrassed," and an ancient Latin one, which means "put to death," which it seemed a little late for.

"I can keep looking," I told her.

"Thank you, California, but I believe this job is bigger than the both of us." She pulled her phone from her pocket and had me dial the Magic Maids again. Turns out they have a side business as Garden Goddesses, and as luck would have it, they'd had a cancellation and would be happy to come to Aunt Monica's house on Tuesday. I knew because I could hear the Goddess lady talking loud on the other side of the phone. Cell phones aren't so good for privacy, I've noticed.

Maybe Aunt Monica noticed too, because she walked back up toward the house and sat on the porch swing and finished making all the arrangements out of earshot. Which gave me a chance to talk to Dog a little longer, too, telling him what a good dog he was and how I'd take any more papers he might find, but how he didn't have to find any either, that I'd still think he was special and talented, and any person would be proud to call him their own.

"Thanks for waiting for me earlier," I told Dog. "I was writing to my dad, is all." And then I told him my plan about Dad moving in with me and Aunt Monica and how he'd work at ClayCation and how, if I had my way, we'd never move anyplace else and Dog could be my dog forever.

And if you don't think that matters to him, then you don't know anything about anything.

Dog and I stayed outside for a long while, looking for letters or pretending to, until Aunt Monica called me inside, asking for help.

"It seems the Magic Maids unearthed even more treasure," she told me when I got to the kitchen. They'd not only cleaned the inside of the refrigerator, they'd taken account of the cupboards, too, digging up three bags of wavy noodles, a half dozen cans of beans, and a big jar of nearly expired mushroom soup. "I believe between the two of us, we may be able to construct a supper that does not require ketchup."

You ever use a can opener? I hadn't either, and I kind

of made a mess of things, splashing beans on the sparkly clean counter, but Aunt Monica didn't holler or swat me or get mad at all. She just showed me where the sponges were for wiping such things up. She's got a patient side, Aunt Monica does. At least when it comes to supper.

"What now?" I asked once I'd gotten everything opened and wiped. Aunt Monica said she wasn't quite sure, but we boiled some water and cooked some noodles and dropped the beans in a different pot with some of the mushroom soup, and then I got the idea of crumbling a hunk of meatloaf into that, and Aunt Monica said, "Why not?" and danged if we didn't surprise ourselves by making something worth eating.

Better than Aunt Isabelle's unfrozen meatloaf, anyway.

And then Aunt Monica showed me about putting leftovers in a Tupperware and running a dishwasher, and somewhere in there she started talking about a time when she and Milton were newlyweds and she put shampoo in the dishwasher, thinking it would be the same thing as dish soap, and how there were so many bubbles they sloshed out onto the kitchen floor and down the hallway. Made her laugh, telling that story. And then I laughed and then she touched her hand to my shoulder, just for a second, like I was somebody she didn't mind having around after all.

And then, as I was reaching a can of beans back up into a high cupboard for her, Aunt Monica said, "What would I do without you?"

I thought a whole bunch of things at once then, but mostly I thought about how, if my dad got a job at ClayCation, Aunt Monica wouldn't have to do without me at all.

"Aunt Monica," I said, remembering my letter. "Aunt Monica, do you have any more stamps?"

"California," she said. "California, I believe I do." She wasn't teasing me. I don't know if you can tell that by reading, but she wasn't. She was playing, like we were having a game of tennis or two square, just bouncing good feelings back and forth to each other.

Aunt Monica pulled open what I know used to be a junk drawer, but the Magic Maids had straightened that too. It took a little bit of rooting around to find what she wanted, and meanwhile she had some exciting news to share.

"Mrs. Pilkington, the special collections archivist from the Detroit Public Library, called this afternoon about Eleanor's papers. She wants to see them and invited us to her office Wednesday afternoon. Isn't that wonderful?"

I told her it was. "But how are we going to get there? Does Bradley know how to drive a stick shift?"

"Bradley has his own car, but he will not be driving us. My other good news is that early that same morning I have an appointment"—Aunt Monica paused her stamp searching long enough to wave her hand over her cast arm—"to have this removed. No more showers with my arm wrapped in plastic. No more begging Bradley for rides to the doctor's office. No more needing *you* to type all my correspondence," she said, laughing again. "You must be as eager as I am for this appointment."

I don't quite know how to tell you what I felt hearing that. Sort of like a door was slamming and sort of like something strong was breaking and sort of like nothing at all.

If Aunt Monica had her cast off, I wouldn't be of use to her anymore.

And if I wasn't any use to her anymore, how long until she sent me back to Aunt Isabelle?

I needed to send my dad that letter. I needed to get that stamp and send him that letter and get him here and working at ClayCation before—

"You know, I think it is very kind of you to have written so many letters to Isabelle," Aunt Monica went on, "given that she's been the source of our meatloaf misery."

What did she say? Letters to Aunt Isabelle? "You mean the bread-and-butters?" I asked.

"Those, yes, but really all of them. The Magic Maids showed me the pile of letters you'd written, before they put them in the mailbox."

I'm sure there's something in *Proper Manners for Proper Ladies* about saying "excuse me" or "pardon me" or "I have to use the ladies' room" before you go tearing away from a conversation and outside to a mailbox, but I don't know that book so well, and even if I did, I don't think I'd have been able to stop myself.

The mailbox was empty.

Of course it was. Be dumb to think it wouldn't be.

Be dumb to hope Aunt Monica had been wrong and go check under the guest room bed, but I did that, too.

My Bella letters were gone, just in case you had any doubt.

The Magic Maids had mailed my letters.

All those letters about my dad and the Official Meeting and the Land of Milk and Honey. All the wishes and secrets. All of them.

Gone.

Not gone, actually.

Not burned up or buried or dusted or final-resting in a passed-on world.

My letters were gone to Minnesota, which was worse.

They were on their way to Aunt Isabelle, who would read them and think the same things about me that the Official Meeting lady did about how hard it must be living with me and with my hormones and my girl needs and all the rest.

And she'd tell Aunt Monica.

And then, soon as Aunt Monica's arm got uncasted, and she could open her own bean cans, and type her own letters,

and drive her own stick-shift car,

she'd be taking me back to Aunt Isabelle's,

or to some other city to live with some other person who didn't know yet about my wishes and secrets and hormones and needs.

And I'd be gone too.

And just as I was thinking this, Aunt Monica knocked on the guest room door, saying she'd found the stamps and did I want them. And I had to make my voice normal and not like somebody who'd been crying or something like that and say could she just leave them in the kitchen, please?

"Are you okay?" Aunt Monica asked. "Do you need anything?"

I need a lot of things. I'm guessing you've figured that out by now.

I didn't tell her that, though. I just said no, and then I was quiet and she was quiet, and after a while I guess she went away, and I was just sitting there twisting up a bed pillow, thinking how if Miss Tenzing was here, she wouldn't even need to see the detonation sign, she'd just know.

And then I heard a throat-clearing behind me.

Last thing I needed was a lecture on sitting up straight and using a handkerchief.

"Leave me alone, Eleanor," I said to her.

"I'll leave you alone when you set down that pillow-case. Who do you think's going to have to mend that?" Her voice was different. Younger, sure, but something else, too. I turned around to get a look and there she was, tall as ever, but scrawnier, too, and wearing an apron, of all things. Her hair was frizzed up around her face, which was red and tired and a little sweaty, but the longer I looked, the more I saw the kid in it.

"Didn't anybody ever tell you staring's rude?" she asked. "And who are you calling Eleanor?"

34

"Elsie?" I said.

"California?" she said. "What's the matter with you? You look like you've seen a ghost."

You know I kept the truth of that to myself. "I . . . I'm surprised to see you, is all," I said.

"Seems like it." Her accent was pure Kansas. Least I think it was. Wasn't British, that's for sure.

"Elsie Cooper," I said. I could hardly believe it. "I . . . hello."

"I hello you, too," she said. "You get into your aunt's tonic or something?"

I shook my head.

"You want to tell me what's got you so upset? Or should I just lend you my mending needle so you can fix that case on your own?"

I set down the pillow and reminded myself not to stare. "How old are you?" I asked.

"You know I'm twelve," she said. "Or did you mean how old does Van Hoeven think I am? Everybody here thinks I'm fifteen—don't you mess up and tell them different."

I shook my head again, letting her know I wouldn't.

"You don't talk much, do you?" Elsie said.

"You don't usually give me the chance," I told her.

Elsie flickered then—just a little around the hairline, but I saw it.

"Don't go," I said. Came out a little loud.

"I'm not going anyplace. I got Van Hoeven and the rest convinced I'm slow at room cleaning, but I'm faster than all of them put together. I just play slow so I can take breaks here and there." She'd made her way over to the desk chair and was taking a seat, leaning back, crossing her feet up on the desk, which I didn't have to study *Proper Manners for Proper Ladies* to know was not considered the best of etiquette. I didn't mind, though. Made me feel like she was settling in, like she'd be staying awhile. "Now," she said, "are you going to tell me what's so awful it's got you tormenting the linens?"

35

And just like that, I started telling Elsie everything,
stepping careful around any fact that might dust her.

I told her about the Magic Maids and about the letters
I never intended to send.

I told her those letters had secrets and wishes in them.

And then I told her what the secrets and wishes were—
about my dad and the Land of Milk and Honey and the
Official Meeting.

Told her a lot of things that weren't in my Bella letters
too, stuff I didn't say at the Official Meeting, either, or to
Miss Tenzing, no matter how kindly she asked. I told Elsie
about how it was every day, not knowing when my dad

would be home from work or who might be with him and what sort of mood they might be in. I told her about strangers drinking beer and sleeping on the couch, and lady friends getting angry, and stuff I don't want to burden you with right now, if you don't mind.

I didn't tell her that my mom was dead (dusting concerns), but I did say she was gone and that I missed her.

It felt good telling Elsie all those things, if you want to know the truth.

But I still didn't want Aunt Isabelle knowing them.

"Maybe you could steal your letters back," Elsie said. "How far's Minnesota? You think you can get there before those letters do?"

"I can't drive a stick shift," I said. "Plus, I'm eleven."

"I could drive a horse cart by nine," Elsie said in a way that made me see the Eleanor in her. Not mean or anything. Just Eleanor.

"You know anybody in Minnesota who could steal those letters for you?" she asked.

I told her I didn't.

"You got telegram money? If you telegrammed your aunt Isabelle, saying, 'Do not read those letters,' you think she'd listen?"

I didn't tell Elsie I didn't think people sent telegrams anymore. I just said how when I was sending Aunt Isabelle the bread-and-butters, she hadn't written back, even when I'd asked her to. "Elean—" I started, but then I caught myself. "*Somebody* I know said Aunt Isabelle probably wasn't reading my letters in the first place."

"Maybe she won't read these, either." Elsie turned her head like she'd heard something. "Dang bell. Somebody told Van Hoeven how in England people have bells to call their maids, and now he's ringing one every time he needs his back scratched. I have to go."

"Thanks for your help," I said. "Thanks for listening."

Elsie snorted. "If I hadn't, you'd have torn that case to shreds!" She dropped her feet from the desk and smoothed out her apron. Then she got serious. "I'm your friend, California. Friends do what's best for each other."

And then that maid bell must have rung again, because Elsie rolled her eyes and said "Coming, m'lord" in an accent that was a little bit British and a little bit not, and then she popped away.

You noticed what she said, right? That she was my friend?

I had never thought of Eleanor as a friend, exactly, but Elsie?

And just like that, I knew it could be true if I wanted it to be.

As long as Elsie doesn't dust, we can be friends. Best friends, even.

For as long as I'm at Aunt Monica's.

Thinking that reminded me all over again about my letters and Aunt Isabelle and how I had to stop her from reading them. I didn't have a telegraph, and while I thought about borrowing Aunt Monica's phone, seemed like if I did, she might start asking a lot of questions, and as I said, I'm not always the best at answering.

My options, as you must have figured already, were limited.

Dear Aunt Isabelle,
   Some letters got mailed to you today by accident. Please don't read them.
   Sincerely,
   California Poppy

PS—If you already did read them, could you please not tell Aunt Monica about them? You can just throw them away or send them back if you want. I'm enclosing some extra stamps, just in case.

PPS—We had another one of your meatloaves yesterday and it was really good. I hope you win the contest.

PPPS—I know you don't like writing back much, but if you can't send the letters back, could you at least write and say you promise you won't read them?

PPPPS—Or if you did read them, could you write and say that you won't tell anybody about them?

PPPPPS—I know it says in Proper Letters *that writing a bunch of PS's is proof the writer is scatterbrained or desperate, but I'm just fine and there is nothing to worry about.*

37

I used my most important-looking calligraphy on Aunt Isabelle's please-don't-read-those-other-letters letter, got a Forever stamp from the book Aunt Monica had left in the kitchen, and went out to the mailbox. Soon as I raised the little red flag on the mailbox, Dog was there, jumping and spinning and barking his little gaspy bark.

"Good to see you, Dog," I said, and he looked back at me like he would have said, *Good to see you, too, California*, if he had the voice for it.

He had another paper scrap with him.

"Whatcha got, Dog?" I asked. I put out my hand

and he dropped the scrap straight in, like this was another of the tricks he'd learned just for me. Despite the almost-there slobber, I could tell the paper was the expensive kind, thick and heavy and made for having important words on it. Looked like it was the second or third page of something, because the words started midsentence.

your father knew all. I am enclosing all proof of my early life for you to do with what you will. Burn it or publish it or toss it to the wind if you like, but understand this: My mistake was not in hiding my past, but in allowing you to grow up believing that the gifts to which you were born—health, wealth, and opportunity— make you superior to others, including your own mother, and that compassion is a lesser virtue than status and position.

You have made clear that my counsel is unwelcome. "Share your advice with someone who cares," were your exact words, I believe, and I have taken them to heart. It may be that I have something to share with those who were not born into the world you were, but who deserve the respect and opportunity that come with knowing the rules of that world and choosing for themselves when to follow them.

*You may, dear boy, have done more good than
the harm you wished to inflict.*

Sincerely,

Mother

*PS—I have returned to this letter because
I cannot sign off in anger or resentment. In
your most recent correspondence you made
clear that you planned never to see me again.
If this is to be our good-bye, I want you to be
absolutely certain of one thing: Whether you
and your brother claim me as your mother or
not, you will always be my children and I will
always love you.*

*PPS—And now I am thinking of the joyful
possibility that you may someday have children
of your own and understand.*

PPPS—Let your children have a dog.

I had to read that scrap four times before I understood
it. And not because the words were big or the writing
was old-fashioned or anything like that. It was just that
I couldn't figure how anybody could decide that being
without a mom who loved them was better than being
with one.

Made me feel bad for Eleanor. And like maybe I shouldn't have dusted her all those times. She was doing her best, is what I was thinking. When a person does their best, seems like other people should keep them around, is all.

38

For the next few days I kept myself busy, mostly by making sure Aunt Monica didn't forget how helpful it was having me around.

I took things off high shelves for her,

and carried things from one place to another for her,

and dialed numbers on the phone for her every time she needed me to, which was a lot.

Seemed the closer Aunt Monica got to being free of her cast, the more she wanted to be on that phone making appointments and talking to people about things she said I didn't need to stick around for.

I did other things for her too, like writing thank-you

notes even though she didn't ask me to. (That's called taking initiative.)

You'd be surprised how many thank-you notes you can write when you put your mind to it, especially if you're thinking about things somebody else could be grateful for.

I wrote one to Bradley for calling the ambulance when Aunt Monica fell,

and I wrote one to the ambulance people for taking her to the hospital,

and I wrote one to the Magic Maids for making everything smell like Christmas lemons,

and I wrote one to the mail lady saying how it must be a lot of work carrying everybody else's thank-you notes around and not ever getting one yourself.

I even wrote a thank-you letter to Mrs. Pilkington of the Detroit Public Library, thanking her for making an appointment with us, but Aunt Monica said that might be overdoing it and maybe I should wait until after we actually met with Mrs. Pilkington on Wednesday before we did our thanking.

In between all the reaching and carrying and thanking, I kept a close eye on the mailbox, just in case Aunt Isabelle responded to my note. I checked so often Elsie said she feared I'd wear out the no-color carpet with all my walking back and forth. "You should just move your writing desk under the window if you want to look out so much," she said.

I thought she was joking. It wasn't even my desk, it was Aunt Monica's. Seemed like the worst kind of manners to rearrange the furniture of a room you were only supposed to be a guest in, but then Elsie said how I was also wearing *her* out with all my pacing, and if I didn't move the desk, she would.

Last thing I needed was Elsie getting gung ho about lifting a lamp, then watching her hand pass through it and dusting herself into nothing.

"No," I said. "I'll do it."

"I can help," Elsie said, but I told her to sit on the bed and rest. (Don't ask me why sitting on real-world things was something she could do, but picking them up or moving them wasn't. The passed-on world is a puzzle I don't have the box picture for.)

"You can help by keeping me company," I told her, which was not a lie.

Ever since she'd turned twelve, Elsie'd become real good company, popping in to tell me about the fierce Irish cook who slept with a butcher knife under her pillow, or how Van Hoeven colored his hair with shoe polish, or about the fancy hotel guests who came from all different places but a lot of times you couldn't tell until they spoke, and how Elsie had to bite the inside of her cheek to stop herself from imitating their accents every time they said hello.

The hotel's latest guest, Elsie was saying, was a

Massachusetts gentleman who kept talking about "pah-king himself in a dining cahr" for the train ride west. I could tell that story was going to be a long one, so while she was talking in her Massachusetts way, I started moving my writing things careful to the top of the dresser. Turned out the desk wasn't as heavy as it looked. Only took a minute to drag it across the carpet and nudge it into place under the window.

Elsie interrupted her story long enough to nod her approval. "Better," she said. (Came out like "Bettah.") "But now it's crowding your nightstand."

I took a look at the nightstand. Elsie was right. It needed moving too.

The nightstand was smaller than the desk, but it was a lot heavier, and I had to take the drawers out to move it. One of those drawers held a pretty pink quilt with embroidery flowers and ribbon trim, and soon as I saw it, I knew it was too fine for shoving back in a drawer. Spread it across the foot of my bed instead.

And then, with the nightstand in its new spot, the lamp needed moving too. And then the chair. And then the wicker laundry basket. And pretty soon everything but the bed had been moved and straightened and set out in new places that looked like maybe that was how they'd belonged in the first place.

Once that was done, seemed safe to put my writing things back on the desk. The Proper Ladies books were better suited for the nightstand, and I stacked them pretty too.

"Manners," Elsie said. Then she snorted. Don't know which surprised me more.

"What's wrong with manners?" I asked.

"There's nothing wrong with them, I guess. It just depends on how you use them. And why," she said. "Manners are like those fancy fish forks we set out at supper. They make it easier to eat trout, but they'll also make a good-size stab hole if a person's so inclined."

I waited quiet, hoping Elsie'd have a story attached to that example, but she didn't. Instead she started singing one of the songs the hotel cook loved, the one about the girl who was a fishmonger and whose parents had been in the same line of work, and how even after the girl was dead, her ghost was still stuck wheeling a cart around Ireland, trying to sell her cockles and her mussels and whatnot.

"You think it works that way?" Elsie asked. "When you die?"

I told her I hoped that people in the passed-on world had better things to think about than seafood.

What I didn't say, but I was also starting to hope, was that most passed-on people had it better than Elsie did. Didn't seem fair, her spending forever just cleaning and scrubbing and being manners'd at by people who were fish-fork rude.

Seemed like if the universe was going to go to all the trouble of having a passed-on world, it should be a little more fun than that.

Before I could think much more about it, though, Elsie gasped. The sunlight had shifted and was beaming through the window, hitting the blue ink bottle, bouncing tiny rainbows all over the no-color walls and the pink flower quilt and the Proper Ladies books and everywhere anyone could see.

"It's lovely," Elsie said.

It was.

"Your whole room is lovely," she went on. "Like you. Like it belongs to you now. Like you belong in it."

I shook my head. I did. But I'll tell you something else—I put those boxes of mine away in Aunt Monica's closet. Closed the door on them too.

And when I did, one of those little ink bottle rainbows hit the mirror on that door, and I swear to you—whole truth—looking through it was like seeing myself and somebody else at the same time.

39

And then, Tuesday morning, the Garden Goddesses appeared.

There were a half dozen of them, all different ages, wearing Garden Goddess T-shirts and pretty green gloves, and carrying tools for cutting and raking and making things nice. They talked a little with Aunt Monica about what she wanted and what they could do, and then they set in to working, steady and quiet and like there was no place else they'd rather be.

For a long while Aunt Monica and I sat on the back porch, watching them work. We told each other we were there in case the Goddesses turned up something for IMPORTANT—FAMILY, but really I think it was because it was a beautiful thing watching that garden turn back into itself. When Dog showed up, he must have felt the same, because rather than wiggling and wanting to run, he just sat on my foot and leaned his almost-there self against my leg. Sometimes, when Aunt Monica wasn't looking, I'd sneak my hand over and give him an almost-there scratch.

I believe I could have sat there all day watching that transformation.

That was the word Aunt Monica used. Transformation.

Or maybe she said it was transformative?

It was one of those times when things felt possible, is what I'm saying.

Anyway, we sat there for a long while, quiet and watching, and neither of us heard the mail lady come up to the gate until she said, "Knock, knock," and, "Is there a California Poppy living here?"

Aunt Monica said there was and the mail lady held up a big box.

"This is for you," she said to me.

My first thought was that Aunt Isabelle had returned my letters. I jumped to my feet, which—I'm sorry to say— sent Dog running, but I couldn't help it. I didn't want Aunt Monica asking about the box and what was in it and could she see?

"I'm going to take this inside," I told her quick. "Be right back."

Elsie was in my room when I got there. "What's that?" she asked.

"Not sure," I said. I smoothed out the pink quilt and set the box down on it. It was a lot bigger than it needed to be for returning letters.

Was a lot bigger than it needed to be for a thinking-of-you gift of Alaska salmon, too, which was my second guess.

Turned out the person thinking of me wasn't Aunt Isabelle or my dad.

It was Ms. Kate Ruby, assistant marketing director of the Playpax Corporation.

Ms. Kate Ruby had sent along a whole big box full of tampons and pads. She'd tucked a note inside, too.

Ms. Kate Ruby's note said thank you for my letter and that she had read it and she didn't know whether I used pads or tampons but she was sending me enough of both to keep me from having to walk to the Chuckles for a whole year. Said she'd sent some extra, too, in case I had friends in the same situation.

I didn't really have any friends like that, as you know. I mean, I liked Salma at ClayCation a lot, but I wasn't sure we had the kind of relationship for bringing a spare box of tampons to. Didn't think Elsie'd be interested either, but turns out I was wrong about that and she had all kinds of questions. They didn't have videos at her school, of course, and didn't anybody talk about stuff like periods at her house, either. Ms. Kate Ruby had put a brochure in the big box, though, so I showed Elsie that diagram about the uterus and ovaries, and she was real glad to know about them and what they do.

I know a lot of people would say it's not polite to talk about this stuff, but when Elsie's first period comes, she's not going to be scared by it, and I don't think even old Eleanor would call that impolite.

Friends do what's best for each other, is what I'm saying.

The other thing Kate Ruby said in her letter was that I was full of good ideas, and she hoped when I was old enough, I would contact her and maybe someday I'd be working at the Playpax Corporation too.

Elsie clapped her hands. "A work offer already! California, you're so lucky! You're going to get out of here and go places. And I'm going to be stuck my whole life cleaning rooms and getting yelled at by Van Hoeven."

I wanted to tell her she wouldn't. I wanted to tell her she'd grow up and marry Fletcher Fontaine and have boys and write books.

Except doing that might dust her.

And also, I was beginning to wonder if her ghost self actually would grow up. For the last few days she'd been telling me about the work she was doing at the hotel, and either it was the same thing every day, or else she was living the same day over and over.

Now that I think of it, maybe there isn't much difference.

Like I said before, I'm not sure how the passed-on world works.

All I know is that as long as she is twelve and I'm eleven, she can take her breaks with me and we can tell stories and sing songs and share secrets.

I can be her friend and she can be mine.

Anything else, I don't want to think about.

What I *do* want to think about is how this might be the best truth possible.

How it might be that Elsie never dusts again and will always be my friend.

How Aunt Isabelle might never read my letters.

How it might be that Aunt Monica keeps right on needing me here.

How Salma and her mom might keep thinking they need an employee, and how they might never see any of the trouble in me, and how Dad might come back and everything could be okay.

How if I just stand here quiet, and don't move and don't breathe, nothing will change.

40

Thing is, you have to breathe. If you want to be alive, anyway.

And you have to eat, too, which I hadn't done yet that afternoon, so I asked Elsie to come with me to the kitchen, and she said she would, even though she wasn't hungry just then.

I thought Aunt Monica'd still be outside with the Goddesses, but soon as we left the guest room, I could hear that she wasn't.

I could hear she was in the study, talking on her phone. I could hear the voice of the person she was talking with too.

"Listen," the voice said. "Listen."

I must have lost my balance then, because next thing, I was sitting on the hallway floor, Elsie crouching over me. "What are you doing? You bump into something? You get the wind knocked out of you?"

"Shhhh," I said.

"Listen," I heard Aunt Isabelle say again, "Davis told her he was going to Alaska. What was I supposed to say? 'Your daddy drinks too much. He's checking himself into some sort of center'? She's eleven, you know."

"What's a center?" asked Elsie.

"Shhh," I said. "Shhh."

"If you think it's so important, *you* tell her," I heard Aunt Isabelle say. "And while you're at it, tell her to stop sending me mail. I'm up to my elbows in raw hamburger, and I don't have time for make-believe and lies."

"Shh," I said again. "Please, shhhh."

"I didn't say anything," said Elsie.

Aunt Isabelle kept talking and talking and I couldn't do anything to stop her.

I just sat there on the floor like a pile of nothing.

"Her letters are full of stories," Aunt Isabelle said.

"Lies," she said.

"She just wants attention," she said. "She's even claiming there's a ghost in your house."

Elsie's eyes got wide and she turned so pale I could have read a newspaper through her. "What did she say?"

Elsie was flickering. Felt like I was flickering too. Felt

like any second one or the other of us was going to dust for good.

"Come on," I said quick. I reached for Elsie's hand, but my fingers went through her, and she flickered worse than before. "Come with me," I said, loud enough to drown out any other stupid words Aunt Isabelle might be saying, and then we were running down the hall and through the kitchen and out the back door and into the garden, and it felt so good to run and run, and I would have kept running, but there were Goddesses everywhere I looked, chopping up dirt and tearing up weeds and ripping out all the things that didn't belong.

I wanted to smash their clippers and snap their rakes. I wanted to snatch up a flowerpot and dash it on the cement and watch the pieces skitter.

"Your hand okay?" Elsie asked.

I was making Miss Tenzing's detonation sign, even though there was no Miss Tenzing around to see it.

"I have to get out of here," I said.

Elsie nodded.

"Promise me you won't eavesdrop while I'm gone. Promise me you'll be here when I get back," I said.

"Of course I'll be here," Elsie said. "Where would I go?"

"Where does anyone go?" I asked her back.

I ran before she could think about answering.

41

I ran and ran, all the way to ClayCation, all the way to the door, all the way inside. There wasn't any birthday party going on, but there was a table of ladies chatting together, painting fancy teacups, and it was all I could do to not run up and slap the cups from their hands, just to hear them shatter.

Might have, if Naomi hadn't come out of the back room just then. "California," she said. And then Salma came out too. "Hey, California," she said.

"I came for my pot," I told them both.

I was going to take it behind the MiniMart. I was going to smash it—lid and all—against the MiniMart wall. I was going to smash it and shatter it, and then I was going to pick up the big pieces and smash them again, and step on what was left, and leave the whole mess for Randy the Cashier to sweep up, and he'd tell Salma and Naomi he'd known I was no good, and they'd all know he was right.

Didn't tell Salma and Naomi that, though. Just said I'd come for the coil pot and could I have it.

Naomi saw something in me then, I guess.

"Do you have a minute?" she asked. "Could you help with something?"

I didn't have a minute. I didn't.

"Okay," I said.

Naomi nodded to Salma, and without them having to say any words to each other, Salma knew what her mama meant and dragged me back to the EMPLOYEES ONLY room and showed me this big brick of clay—big enough for a dozen pots and hard as a frozen meatloaf.

"There's a whole bunch of senior ladies coming in a half hour," Salma said. "I'm supposed to soften this up for them."

And then she showed me how to do that.

How to drop the clay on the table

and pound it down with your fists

and fold it over

and pound it again

and again

and again.

Turns out, I'm real good at softening clay bricks.

Good enough that when Naomi came into the EMPLOY-EES ONLY room and saw what I'd done, she said that thing again about me working there someday and how I could stay and help with the senior ladies if I wanted.

"I can't," I said, "I have to go." Took a couple of steps toward the door then, too, but Salma stopped me.

"You can't go without your pot," she said.

I told her it was okay, I didn't need that pot anymore.

Truth was, I didn't feel like smashing things anymore.

I didn't feel like anything.

"I don't have room in my boxes for it," I told her. "I don't know what I'd do with it."

But Salma'd tucked around a corner shelf and was already heading back to me. She was holding this big, lumpy cocoon-looking thing—a swaddle of newspaper and tape. "We were going to mail it to you," Salma said. "Mom wrapped it up so it wouldn't break."

And then she set the swaddled-up pot in my arms, gentle as if it were a living thing.

It was heavier than it looked.

More solid, too.

For half a second I feared I'd drop it, which right then was the last thing I wanted.

I was not going to smash that pot.

I was not going to leave it behind, either.

I didn't know what I was going to do with it, but

feeling the weight of this thing I'd made in my arms, I knew for sure I wasn't going to leave it behind.

"Open it," Salma said. "It came out great. You should see it."

It wasn't that I didn't want to see it.

It wasn't.

It's just, Naomi'd gone to all the trouble of swaddling it and taping it, and it was protected, is all.

"I'll see it later," I said.

"I have to go," I said.

"Thank you," I said.

"You're welcome," Salma said. Sounded like she meant it.

"You will always be welcome," Naomi said. She meant it too, I could tell. Even if I was dumb or troublesome or set to detonate, Naomi was saying I was welcome.

And then, for a second, I thought she was going to hug me, but turned out she was meaning to pat the pot in my arms instead. Still, Naomi looked at me straight on, in that mom way I'd seen her look at Salma.

"Take care," she said.

I still don't know if she meant for me to take care of me or for me to take care of the pot, but right then, with that pot all swaddled and hugged up safe, I couldn't help remembering what Salma said about things we make having a little bit of us mixed up in them, and it felt like maybe there wasn't much difference.

42

When I got back to Aunt Monica's, the Garden Goddesses truck was gone.

I opened the house door real careful and went straight to the guest room and set the swaddled pot gentle on the guest room bed, between a pillow and one of Kate Ruby's tampon boxes. Thought about opening it to look inside, but then, just like that, Elsie was there.

"Your aunt's out back," she told me. "She's been talking on that telephone thing of hers all afternoon, but I didn't get near enough to hear a word, I swear."

You might find it hard to believe, but ever since Salma handed me that swaddle, I'd almost forgotten about Aunt

Isabelle telling Aunt Monica all those things about me.

"You think she's still talking to Aunt Isabelle?" I asked.

"I told you I didn't listen." Elsie sounded a little miffed. "I keep my promises, you know."

I told her I believed her.

"Okay," Elsie said. She fiddled with her apron then. Fussed with her hair a little, too. "But . . . well . . . I didn't hear a *word*, but I did kind of hear the *way* she was talking. You know how if you listen at a hotel door, you can't really hear *what* people are saying, but you can tell if they're happy or angry or wishing they were someplace else?"

I've never even been inside a hotel, but I'd heard enough through the walls at my dad's to understand. I nodded. "Did she sound angry?" I asked.

"She sounded like she was making plans."

I didn't say anything after that. What was there worth saying? I was pretty sure Elsie knew as well as I did that Aunt Monica was making plans to send me back to Isabelle's. Probably helping Isabelle figure out where to send me after that.

"Your dad didn't tell you he was going to a . . . what'd she say? Center?" Elsie said when the quiet got to be too much.

"I think Aunt Isabelle meant a rehab center or something like that," I said. "And no, he didn't."

Elsie nodded. "Is he mean when he drinks? Your dad?"

I told her he wasn't. That he was a good dad and a

kind dad, but he wasn't always a right-there-when-you-needed-him sort.

"You miss him?" she asked.

"I do," I said. "A lot. You miss your dad?"

"Not a lick. Don't miss anybody back home, except Oakley."

I remembered Eleanor mentioning somebody named Oakley before. "Was he a friend at school?" I asked.

Elsie laughed. "Oakley was my dog. Best dog you ever met, too. Sweet and soft and smart as smart."

I know you figured it out already.

Truth is, I had too. I just hadn't wanted to.

I can believe a lot of dumb things if I want to, is what I'm saying.

Like an aunt might not read my letters if I asked her not to,

or a dad might be going to Alaska just to do some fishing,

or rainbows might mean I belonged in a place,

or an almost-there dog might show up among the garden flowers just to be with me.

"He could sit and stay and roll over and play dead," Elsie went on. "He'd shake and bark on command, and he could jump through hoops, too, like it was nothing."

She said it like she could still see him doing those things. Like she was still with him. Like being there with him was the only real thing in her world, and I swear, for a minute, she was solid as you or me. "I could have stayed with that pup all day, every day, if it weren't for needing to hide him from my pa," she said. "Every time I left to do chores or go to school, I felt bad about it, but I promised Oakley I'd be back, and sure enough, next day I'd find him there, waiting. I'll tell you what, California, I'd go back home in an instant if I could see Oakley again. It's the one thing I feel sort of bad about."

Elsie had a truly sad look on her face that I hadn't seen before. Not even when she was Eleanor. "It wasn't your fault that you had to leave," I told her.

Elsie said a curse word then, which I know her Eleanor self wouldn't have approved of. "I didn't even know I was leaving. Pa told me to chase Oakley off, but I hadn't done it yet, and when he called me to the wagon, I told Oakley, 'Stay,' and promised I'd come right back, but I didn't. I got in Pa's wagon and he drove me here, and you know the rest."

I did.

I knew more of the rest than she did.

"I never did have time to tell him what a good dog he was or to say good-bye or thank you," Elsie said. "Wish I could have said thank you. Seems only—"

"Proper," we said at the same time.

"If I'd known it was going to be the last time I'd see him," Elsie said, "I'd have said something different, you know?"

I did know.

"What would you have said?" I asked her. "If you had the chance?"

"I'd have said he was the best dog ever. I'd have said I loved him. I'd have told him to go on and have fun and meet some other kid who could feed him and play with him and teach him new tricks."

I nodded.

"I'd have told him that the best days I ever had were right there in our yard, just me and him, and that I'd never forget him and . . . this is going to sound selfish," Elsie said.

I didn't say anything then, but I looked at her straight on, like Naomi and Salma had looked at me, so she'd know I wasn't judging her or anything.

"I'd have told him I hoped he'd have a good life but that he wouldn't forget me either."

"He didn't," I said.

"How do you know?" Elsie asked, and not in an argument way, more like she hoped I knew something truer than she did.

Now it was my turn for feeling selfish.

I could have told her right then about Dog being in the yard.

I could have said I knew he hadn't forgotten her. That ever since I got here—maybe even before that—he'd been out in the backyard waiting just for her.

That he was probably waiting just for her right then.

I could have.

Except doing so, I feared, would dust her.

And dusting her one more time, I was coming to feel, might be dusting her for the last time too.

You ever fall asleep without knowing it?

Like have you ever been in the backseat on a long car ride with the windows rolled down and the world rushing by and your mom in the front seat humming that song about California girls and you're humming too, and then, just like that, it's dark outside and the air is still, and you're waking up in your own driveway?

And have you ever pretended you were still asleep just so your mom would lift you up out of that car and carry you inside and snug you up in your bed, all the time whispering how if you were awake, she'd tell you how sweet you are and how smart and how good, and humming that same song over and over again?

And you ever wake up the next morning, still in your clothes, still hearing that song, but wondering anyway if every last thing you remember was just some dream you wished into dreaming?

Anyway, I must have fallen asleep even before supper, because next thing I knew, Aunt Monica was tapping on the guest room door and light was coming weak in through the window and it was morning. The pink flower quilt had been laid overtop of me, and Ms. Kate Ruby's tampon boxes had been moved to the desk, but the swaddled pot was still in my arms, and I was hugging it tight like a little kid does a stuffed animal friend.

"California?" Aunt Monica said through the door, almost whispering, almost not. "California? There are bagels on the counter for your breakfast. Bradley's going to take me to the doctor's, but as soon as this is off"—I imagined her doing that game show wave around her cast—"I'll be back, and then we can go downtown for our day, okay?"

I believe I said okay. Hard to tell.

"I have a couple of other errands while we're down there," she said. "And . . . well, there are some things we should talk about."

I probably said okay about that, too, even though it wasn't.

"Can you be ready to go when I get back?"

I told her I could be ready to go.

That much I'm sure about.

Dear Bella,

Maybe it seems strange that I'm writing to you, given the kind of trouble it's gotten me into, but I figure with my hormones and my girl things and everything else, I've got trouble built in anyway. Mostly, though, I don't want Aunt Isabelle being the one putting an end to things instead of me, and seeing as I'm probably going to have to go back there any day now, or to some other aunt's or stranger's or who knows where, I'm not sure my future holds any kind of privacy at all for saying what I need to.

Plus, I'm down to my last few sheets of gray-lined paper. Nearly out of ink, too.

So this is a good-bye letter. See, all those times before—like when my mom died and my dad left and even when Aunt Isabelle dropped me off here—I didn't know enough to say a proper good-bye. This time I want it to be different, though. This time I know what's coming and I have a chance to say what needs saying first.

There's no such thing as a good-bye letter in Proper Letters for Proper Ladies, by the way, but there is a whole section about the close, which is that part of a regular letter where you put an end to things, writing "Sincerely" or "Gratefully" or "Affectionately," but never, Eleanor says, "Warmly yours," which is vulgar and sounds like you're just begging an excuse to take off your wrap.

If you're writing to somebody important, like the President, you can say "Your most obedient servant" at the end, or "Yours faithfully" or "Yours very truly" or "Believe me." Doesn't tell how to say good-bye to somebody important who is not like the President. I looked.

Anyway, I know you're not real or anything, but when I wrote to you all those times before, it felt like you were real and like you were

listening and almost like, sometimes, I could imagine you writing me back, telling me what I should do about things.

Like right now I can imagine you writing me back, saying how if I have only a little bit of paper left, maybe I should be brave and write to someone real—

~

Dear Ms. Kate Ruby,

Thank you for the tampons and pads and for the very nice letter. I'm not sure I would like to work at a tampon company, no offense, but if I ever change my mind, it is good to know who to talk to about career opportunities. I hope you and your team keep working on those ideas, especially the one about having boys watch the movies.

Sincerely,
California Poppy

~

Dear Miss Tenzing,

I have been reading a book called Proper Letters for Proper Ladies that says failing to

thank someone properly for a kindness tells a lot
more about a person than the clothes they wear
or their addresses they keep. My address keeps
changing and some of my clothes are too small,
but I know you never did judge me, and I want
to thank you for that and for seeing the eleven
in me, and the smart in me, and maybe even the
thank-you-writing person in me.

I know on the last day of school I wasn't so
nice. I saw you saying good-bye and giving out
hugs to all the other kids, and right then I did
want a hug and I didn't want to say good-bye
and I couldn't figure out how to get one without
the other, I guess. Anyway, thank you for
everything, and if ever I do see you again, I will
say good-bye properly, and if you want to hug
me then, that would be okay.

Sincerely,

California Poppy

Dear Salma,

Thank you for teaching me how to make a
coil pot and how to put glaze on it and how to
help with birthday parties. I wish I could go to
Abbot Middle School with you and look over the

heads of people for you, and if you needed the Heimlich, I hope you know I would give it to you before Franklin Furwort had a chance. Thank you for saying you are my friend, and for taking more than five seconds to make it true.

You're smart, so probably you already know this, but people don't always get to choose whether they leave or stay in a place, but just because they have to leave where you are doesn't mean they wouldn't rather be with you.

Believe me,

California Poppy

Dear Aunt Monica,

By the time you get this letter, I'll be living somewhere else, I figure. I hope we had a nice in-person good-bye, but sometimes I'm not so good about saying out loud what I should or shouldn't, so it seems like putting it on paper is best.

This is not a thank-you note, by the way. This is a full and proper thank-you letter, and even though it might not be as long as it should be, seeing as I have only one piece of paper left, I want you to know that I understand the breadth *of your generosity and how truly blessed I've been.*

You have a nice, safe house, and the guest room lots of times felt like it was my very own. I liked making mushroom-meatloaf noodles with you, and I liked working on IMPORTANT— FAMILY *with you and being a part of your purpose. Thank you for letting me stay with you while you had your cast on. I hope it doesn't sound mean, but I wish you could have your cast on a lot longer. Forever, maybe.*

Yours faithfully,

California Poppy

PS—In Proper Letters for Proper Ladies, *Eleanor says don't bother writing an apology letter if you can't take responsibility for your actions and if you aren't truly sorry. Which is why this is not an apology letter.*

I packed up my boxes this morning, and when I did, I put a copy of Proper Letters for Proper Ladies *inside, which I guess is like stealing. I take responsibility for that. But I'm not truly sorry. It's just that somebody I know says that every time you make something, you put some of yourself in it, and I can't help feeling like there's a little bit of Eleanor in this book, which might sound dumb to you but I don't think it is. Anyway, as you might have noticed, I'm not so good at saying good-bye, and I'm not ready for saying a complete good-bye to Eleanor just yet.*

Bradley pulled up into the driveway, dropped Aunt Monica off, and then backed up fast like he was afraid she'd break her arm again if he stayed too long.

Aunt Monica waved her cast-free hand. Her arm was pale and wrinkled and scrawny-looking, and for a second I thought she was going to tell me she'd be needing me to stay put for a while longer until she got back up to full strength, but then she said, "Are you ready to go?"

"Almost," I said.

I found Elsie on the back porch, sitting on the swing, eyes closed. The sky was starting to cloud, but the sun was strong enough to shine her face up, and even though she was a whole lot younger than she had been the first time I met her, she looked just as worn out. You're going to think I'm rude, but I didn't say anything for a bit. Just stood there watching her, hoping later I'd remember what she looked like composed this way.

I thought about waiting. I might be at Aunt Monica's for another couple of days. Maybe even a week or two. And I would be lying if I didn't say nearly everything in me wanted Elsie around as long as possible. But the more I looked at her, the more I saw the twelve in her and the tired in her and the wear it was putting on her to pretend neither of those things was true.

Guess Elsie was as good as I was at feeling somebody staring, because right then she opened her eyes.

"Hey, California," she said, warm as that sun on her face. You ever have anybody talk to you that way? Makes it harder to do what you have to do, I'll tell you that much.

"Hey," I said back.

"Don't tell anyone I'm out here. I worked fast so I could have a break, but if anyone finds out, they'll call me to wash that kitchen floor."

I promised her I wouldn't tell a soul, which might have made old Eleanor flicker, but Elsie sat near solid.

"I was looking for that pup you said was out here sometimes," she said. "One of the ladies had a whole plateful of cookies she hadn't touched, so . . ." Elsie put one finger to her lips and showed me the shortbread she'd snuck in her pocket. "I used to have a dog, you know. His name was—"

"Oakley," we said together.

"I told you?" she asked.

"You told me."

"I was teaching him tricks before I left," she said. "Sitting and jumping through hoops and playing dead. He got real good at it."

That playing-dead part seemed like an opening, but I couldn't take it. If you'd ever had to say good-bye to somebody you were 99 percent sure you wouldn't see again, you'd understand.

"I know," is what I said instead.

"Did I tell you that, too?" Elsie shook her head. "I worked hard at home, but nothing's like hotel work, California. I'm so tired I'm forgetting what I've said and what I've done, and I swear I'd forget my own name if people weren't always hollering it."

I noticed her hands then. Red and cracked and blistery. "Lye," she said, and then, like he'd just caught wind of that cookie, Dog came running out from behind the garage, wheezing and barking and turning circles, happy as always.

"You hear something?" Elsie stood and hurried to the garden, arms out like Dorothy Gale has whenever she's looking surprised, like Cinderella in the Disney movie when the Fairy Godmother taps her head and makes a sparkle dress come and she spins and looks down at herself like she can't believe how she's changed. "California?" Elsie called me from the grass. "You coming?"

"No," I said. But I followed her.

She and Dog were standing in almost the same spot, Elsie listening, Dog sniffing round where her feet were, but neither of them really seeing the other yet.

"I have to say good-bye," I told Elsie.

"You're leaving?" The sad on her face was the same as the night old Eleanor told me Fletcher was sick. And when she told me about her boys not inviting her to their weddings, and now that I thought about it, that sad had also been there around the edges of her when she talked about those parties and meetings and times she had to keep people from knowing her whole self.

Seemed cruel of me making her feel that way again, especially after I'd seen her so happy just now, thinking of her Oakley pup.

"I'm not leaving," I said. "You are. I don't know all the details and I could be wrong about this, I could, but I don't think you're coming back."

"Van Hoeven did say something about trading me to a hotel man he knew in Little Rock."

I watched Elsie try making herself brave about it, her voice changing to something like the one I knew belonged to the hotel cook—strong, with a bit of Irish. "I suppose traveling will be good for me. To see new things, meet people. You think I'll meet new people, California? Maybe some nicer ones, like you?"

I told her I believed she would. It wasn't just manners talking either.

Dog gasp-barked again. He smelled Elsie, I was sure of it. And that cookie. But when I looked down at his black-coffee eyes, I could tell he was barking at me, too, knowing better than I did it was time I set things right.

"I'll miss you," I told him. Dog panted, breathing as hard as he had on that day he showed me all his tricks, as he had when we were there together lying in the grass till he slept and I asked him my favor. "If you meet my mom," I told him, "let her know I'm okay."

Elsie thought I was talking to her. "You think your mom's in Arkansas?"

I shook my head and Elsie didn't push. She just said if she ever met anybody with a girl named California, she'd tell her that California was doing good and was a good friend, too. "I'll tell her where to reach you. Be nice to get a letter now and again, wouldn't it?"

I said it would.

And then I told her she'd been a good friend, best I'd ever had, and that the best days I'd ever had were right there in that house with her, but I hoped she would go where she was going and have fun there and be the kid she never got to be.

"I'll never forget you," I said.

And then I did what I had to do, which, if you don't mind, I'd rather not talk about.

And then Elsie was gone.

And then it was just me and Dog, standing there in Aunt Monica's Goddessed-up garden, wind rattling the plant leaves and a chill in the air like rain was coming. Sky got dark, too. Fat clouds turning gray and green, and where the light did bust through, it had the look of knives about it.

"California?" Aunt Monica called from inside the house. "California, I could use your help."

"Stay," I told Dog, and he did.

The IMPORTANT—FAMILY box was on the kitchen table. "Would you mind putting that in the trunk of the car? It seems my arm is still a little weak, and I don't want to drop it. Again."

I told Aunt Monica I'd do that, sure. It really wasn't all that heavy, but it was hard fitting it in the trunk, which was still crowded with all the golf clubs and music and shoes and the other Milton stuff Aunt Monica had planned on donating. I pushed things around until I made space for the box, but even then it was hard closing the trunk lid, which, I'll tell you right now, I didn't do such a good job of.

"All set," I called to Aunt Monica, but she didn't answer, so I came back out of the garage to holler again, and even though the sky was dark and green and gray, I saw something flicker in the yard, something like those dancing lights at Christmas or the way sunlight sparks off a lake. It was Elsie, almost there and almost not, on her knees, laughing, rubbing Dog's belly like they were long-lost pals. Which I guess they were.

I took a step toward them and Dog sat up. Looked at me, ears pricked, head cocked like the first time we met.

"What is it, Oakley?" Elsie asked. She looked in my direction, but she didn't see me.

Which is how I knew for sure she wouldn't be back.

Dog knew too. I could tell by how wild he was wagging and wiggling. He was ready to run. But I'd told him to stay, and he was listening—like he was my very own and wouldn't do a thing without my telling him it was okay.

"Good dog," I said, because he was, and he deserved to hear it. And then I told him he was the best dog I ever knew and that some of the best days I'd ever had were right there in the garden, just me and him. And that I'd never forget him. And that I hoped he'd never forget me. And he understood. "It's okay, Dog," I said. "Go on."

Dog leaped to his paws and spun around twice and took off running. Elsie laughed then, and it sounded like pink nail polish and sunshine and chocolate shakes. "Hold up, Oakley!" she said, running after him. "Wait! Wait for me!"

And that was the last I saw of either of them. Dog racing around and Elsie running after him, weightless as daylight.

And the sun followed them.

And it rained.

46

Aunt Monica had to call me twice before I heard. She needed help closing her umbrella, her right arm being weaker than it had been before she busted it. She was a little shaky all around, actually. Excited, I figured, about fulfilling her purpose and seeing the librarian and being free of her cast after all this time. Maybe about being free of me soon too.

"All set?" she asked when we got into the car.

I said I guessed so. Truth was, I was a little shaky too, but you're smart and I know you figured that out already. Anyway, Aunt Monica turned the key in the ignition, and the car, which had been resting as long as her arm had been, coughed a couple of times before it decided backing out of the garage was an okay thing to do.

"I have to talk with you about something," Aunt Monica said, but then the car made a terrible sound, like its insides were tearing out. "Oh dear. Hold on."

You ever drive a stick shift? It's almost like a regular car. Not that I've ever driven one of those, but I've been in enough to know that in a regular car you use your foot for the gas pedal and the brake pedal, and your hands get used for steering and drinking coffee and checking maps.

With a stick-shift car, it's almost the same, except there are three pedals, so you have to use both feet, and you can't drink coffee or check maps because while your left hand is doing the steering, your right hand is pushing around the stick, which is this crooked-looking rod thing with a ball on the end, and every time you speed up or slow down, you have to push that stick around. And if you don't do it exactly right, the whole car shudders and crunches loud and angry enough to make your teeth ache.

Probably would have sounded even louder if it wasn't for the rain banging on the car roof and the other cars honking and zooming around us at the stoplights, which, Aunt Monica said, they wouldn't be doing except her weak arm was making it hard to push that stick firm as she needed to.

Probably that's why she kept hitting potholes, too.

"Crabs!" she said each time. Or something like it.

And then she'd take a deep breath and start again, saying "So" and "California," but then the rain would get louder or the car would crunch louder, and all the time the potholes were going *whump*, *whump*, *whump*, until finally we hit one that didn't just go *whump*. It went *WHUMP*, and then there was this huge clatter like somebody dropped a whole drawer of silverware.

Aunt Monica said more than "crabs" then.

I turned around. Remember how I said I wasn't so good at shutting that trunk lid? Well, there was the proof of it. That last pothole had popped the trunk wide open and the lid was flapping up and down, up and down, and all of Milton's things—his golf clubs and his brown coat and his music collection and his shoes and his clothes— were spilling out onto the road. And just beyond that, IMPORTANT—FAMILY was tumbling end over end like it was through with us and had someplace else it needed getting to fast.

"Stop!" I yelled, but Aunt Monica was already swerving onto the road shoulder. Next thing, I was out of the car and leaping over the brown coat and dodging the golf clubs and running fast as I could through the rain after that box. The lid was off and Eleanor's letters were swirling up into the wind and out into the road and getting beaten down by the rain and run over by cars, but I didn't slow a step.

"California!" Aunt Monica said, but she didn't need

to. If I ran fast enough, I could catch it. I was sure of it. I could catch it and save whatever part of her purpose was still inside.

"California!" Aunt Monica called again, and I ran faster, but that box kept tumbling over itself away from me. "Stop!" I hollered. "Stay!" And you might think I'm lying, but I swear it is the truth, that box seemed to slow down just a little, and I caught it.

A car swerved past, spraying rain and mess and honking its horn, but it didn't matter.

I'd caught it.

And then Aunt Monica caught me.

"California!" she said, pulling me from the road, which I guess I'd stumbled into.

"California," she said, squeezing my arm, pulling me to her chest, crushing what was left of IMPORTANT—FAMILY between us.

47

It was the police lady who decided we shouldn't go to Detroit today after all.

When she heard how old I was, she said I should go sit inside the stick-shift car while she and Aunt Monica put what they could of Milton's things back in the trunk. She shut the trunk tight for us too and followed Aunt Monica all the way back to her driveway, making sure we didn't have any more trouble.

You don't talk much in a car when you know a police lady is following you, in case you don't know.

Took till we were parked in Aunt Monica's garage and

the police lady was driving away before either of us said a word.

"May I see that?" Aunt Monica said.

She meant IMPORTANT—FAMILY. I was still holding on to it, I guess.

I unwrapped my arms from it and handed it over, and as I did, a manila envelope fell out and slid to the floor.

Aunt Monica gasped. Sounded a lot like Dog, if you want to know the truth. And then she picked up that envelope and held it tight, like it was her sole surviving relative and there was no way she'd let it out of her grasp.

"I'm sorry," I said. "I'm sorry I ruined your purpose."

"What? Ruined my what?"

"Your purpose," I said, nodding at the envelope. "Eleanor's biography." And then I apologized for not shutting the trunk tight enough and for having hormones and difficulties and not being the kind of kid it was easy to see the eleven in, and somewhere in the middle of all that I'd gotten out of the car, I guess, because next thing I knew, I was standing in the yard, taking in the garden flowers. And next thing after that, Aunt Monica was beside me. She didn't say anything at first. Just stood there hugging on that envelope, looking into the garden the same way I was.

It was beautiful, the garden.

Raindrops were clinging to the leaves, and the sun was shining, and the whole garden was sparkling and alive. The Goddesses had cleared away all the weeds, and there was space for all the flowers to spread out and be themselves in. And you could see the small blossoms and the colors that were hidden before. And the stone angel birdbath and even the couple of spots that maybe Dog got into were all smooth and pretty, and it felt like the whole yard was breathing.

"This is the way things looked when Milton was here," Aunt Monica said finally. "Actually, it's prettier now. Milton might have been a little too precious with it, he kept everything so trimmed back. I rather like things taller and fuller. It's a garden with its own mind now."

I looked around. I didn't know anything about garden minds, but I nodded anyway.

Waited for her to tell me she wanted to talk to me.

Waited for her to say it was time for me to go.

"The only thing missing is Milton," is what she said.

It surprised me, which is why I said what I said next. "You want me to get him?" I asked.

If Aunt Monica was the type to dust, that question would have done it for sure.

"What did you say?" she asked.

I couldn't come up with a lie or even a possible truth that would be best, so I just repeated myself. "You want me to get him?"

And then the funniest thing happened, and Aunt Monica looked like she'd swallowed a string of Christmas lights. "Yes," she said. "Would you please?"

So I did. I got the box and opened the lid and there was a whole plastic bag of Milton ashes that I was opening up for her, and I know it might sound strange, but it wasn't. Aunt Monica just said, "Milton, this is California, and she just had the mostly lovely idea. How would you feel about spending some time in the garden?"

And then we both listened for his answer for a bit.

"Did you hear anything?" she asked.

I had to tell her I didn't.

"He never was very chatty," Aunt Monica admitted. "Well, barring a clear message from the Beyond, I guess we will have to make up our own minds about how to proceed." Soon enough, we were both walking slow through the garden, me holding the bag of Milton, and Aunt Monica shaking him out little bit by little bit around all the flowers and plants and the quiet spots you never would have noticed, and her saying, "Don't the gladioli look regal, Milt?" and "How about these salvias?" and "I have no idea what this flower is, but you planted it, so I'm sure you do." Her voice cracked a couple of times and she sniffed a lot. I stayed quiet so she could say whatever needed saying.

Aunt Monica is a careful shaker, turns out, so even when we'd gotten to the very end of the garden, back by the birdbath, there was still a fair bit of Milton in the bag.

"You need help?" I asked.

Aunt Monica looked at the bag. "Probably," she said. Made her laugh to say it, but it wasn't the kind of laugh you're supposed to join in with, I knew. "It gives me a great deal of comfort having Milton enjoying his garden," she said, "but I like thinking he enjoys my company, too. Or maybe I'm just not ready to say good-bye to him entirely. I like having a little bit of Milton around."

I told her I understood that, and she looked right at me and said she believed I did.

"Sorry, dear one, to put you back in that ugly shoe box," she said to the ash bag.

I felt sorry about that too, if you want to know the truth. Which is probably what made me think about my coil pot. Sometimes you don't know you need a thing until you have it, is what I'm saying.

It wasn't easy pulling off all that tape and swaddle, but I did it.

Salma was right when she said I should see it.

It was beautiful.

It was pink and glossy, and with every step I took, a new spot caught the light.

It looked like glass, a little bit.

And like sunshine.

And like fresh-painted fingernails.

"Oh," Aunt Monica said, which told me she thought it was beautiful too.

And I told her I'd made it and then I said, "May I?" which I think Eleanor would have approved of. Aunt Monica didn't say anything, but she nodded, and I took the lid off my pot and rolled Milton's ash bag up tight and slid it inside, and the whole thing fit perfect. Aunt Monica and I were sitting on the porch step by then, and I put the lid on the pot and set it in her lap, and she wrapped her good arm around it tight, sort of like she was hugging the Milton inside.

"You're giving this to me?" Aunt Monica said. It was kind of like a whisper, really.

I nodded. "Maybe there could be a little bit of me around too," I said.

"I don't want a little bit of you around," Aunt Monica said.

Which I knew right off was what she had been wanting to say the whole time we were in the car.

"I want all of you."

I'll admit it. That was a surprise.

"I want all of you," she said again. "I mean, I want you to stay here. To live here with me. I want . . ." She'd set the envelope down on the porch step, but now she picked it up again and handed it to me.

There was not a single Eleanor letter inside.

But there were a whole lot of other papers.

I can read. I know you know that by now. Still, this time, even though I knew most of the words on the page, I wasn't sure I understood what they meant.

"'Legal guardianship,'" I read out loud.

"It means I'd like you to stay here," Aunt Monica said, "while your dad is getting better. You know that's what he's doing, right? You know he left you with Isabelle so he could get better and be a better dad?"

I told her I did know that. And also that I didn't. And so she explained everything, slow and gentle, about how my dad had gone to a treatment center to help him make better choices and how he would be there doing "sober living" for a while. And that while he was doing that, she hoped I would stay with her and let her be the grown-up in my life.

"Did he tell you that you had to do this?" I asked.

"I want to do this. I've wanted to since the moment you got here."

I must have had one of my more skeptical looks on my face.

"Well. Not from the first moment. I wasn't . . . I don't know if you noticed, but I wasn't at my best when you first got here. I was . . . asleep? But you woke me up. You made me remember there was something to be awake for."

I didn't say anything then, and Aunt Monica didn't

make me. She just nodded at the envelope again, and then she sat there with me while I read all the other papers, like the email from Miss Tenzing saying how I was a smart and caring girl who would thrive with attention. And the Official Meeting report saying all the things it had to say—which were mostly about my dad and not about me at all. And then there were the legal form papers that were only partway filled in.

"I was planning," Aunt Monica said, "to visit Milton's former law partner when we were downtown. He was going to help me fill in the rest. I hadn't told you before because I wanted to be sure . . ."

The Official Meeting page was still on the top of the stack. "That I wasn't going to be trouble," I said.

"No! I wanted to be sure that I didn't mess up any paperwork," she said. "I wanted to make sure the court would accept me, that I wouldn't lose you."

"My dad knows about this?" I asked.

Aunt Monica nodded at the papers in my lap again, like there was more for me to read. I turned a few pages and saw that there was.

The very last page was a computer printout of a handwritten letter.

Handwriting I know like I know my own breath.

Dear Monica,
  I have signed the papers and am returning

*them to you. This is not easy. I love that little girl
more than anything in the world, but she deserves
a stable place to be and I can't give her that yet.*

*I wrote a letter to her right after I got here,
explaining everything, but by the time I'd mailed
it to Isabelle, California was already with you.
I've asked Isabelle to forward it. We'll see how
long that takes.*

*You said I should call California or use that
video chat thing, and I think you're right. She
deserves that. But in the meantime, would you
tell her some things for me? Would you tell her I
love her and that I'm working on being the dad
she needs, but for a little while longer you'll be
the best adult in her life? You'll help her make
decisions and make sure she has all the things
she needs?*

*I agree with you, she shouldn't have to be an
adult yet. She should be eleven, like you said.
Let her know that, too, okay? And make sure
she knows that I love her and that none of this is
her fault? She's the best kid, Monica. Make sure
she knows that. The best kid that ever was. If
she wants to talk with me, I'll be here. And if she
doesn't, well, I can't be mad about that, can I? I'll
wait. Tell her I'll wait forever if that's what she
needs. I might not be there in West Bloomfield,*

Michigan, right now, but my heart is there, and I'm
working on getting my mind and body there too.
     What I'm saying is, right now I think
California is exactly where she needs to be.
     Sincerely,
     Davis

I didn't need to read my dad's letter four times to understand it.

Read it five times anyway.

Aunt Monica didn't say anything, but she stayed close enough for me to feel how she was there. How she is going to be there as long as I want her to be. How there is no one else she would rather be with.

You might not know this, but you can only sit side-by-side on a porch step with somebody hugging you for so long before your back starts hurting.

You can hold hands if you want to, though.

You can hold hands for a long, long time.

Acknowledgments

Many thanks to Kate Messner who read the first lines of Callie's story on the day they appeared and continued reading no matter how many times her story dissolved and recomposed. Thanks are due as well to Olugbemisola Rhuday-Perkovich for her insightful questions and unflagging encouragement, to the properly brilliant women of the Ladies Sewing Guild, and to the entire Vermont College of Fine Arts Writing for Children and Young Adults community.

This book exists because of the dedicated work of Reka Simonsen (the opposite of a peacock of an editor), cover artist Charles Santoso, and the entire team at Atheneum. I am grateful to my sneakily sentimental agent, Jennifer Laughran, who understands that every story has a little bit of the author in it.

Finally, thanks to Jack and Claire, my sunshine and chocolate shakes, and to Julio, whose hand has held mine from the start.